PUFFIN BOOKS

GRACE

Morris Gleitzman grew up in England and went to live in Australia when he was sixteen. He worked as a frozen-chicken thawer, sugar-mill rolling-stock unhooker, fashion-industry trainee, department-store Santa, TV producer, newspaper columnist and screenwriter. Then he had a wonderful experience. He wrote a novel for young people. Now he's one of the bestselling children's authors in Australia. He lives in Melbourne, but visits Britain regularly. His many books include *Two Weeks with the Queen*, *Water Wings*, *Bumface*, *Boy Overboard* and *Once*.

Visit Morris at his website:
www.morrisgleitzman.com

Books by Morris Gleitzman

The Other Facts of Life
Second Childhood
Two Weeks with the Queen
Misery Guts
Worry Warts
Puppy Fat
Blabber Mouth
Sticky Beak
Gift of the Gab
Belly Flop
Water Wings
Wicked! (with Paul Jennings)
Deadly! (with Paul Jennings)
Bumface
Adults Only
Teacher's Pet
Toad Rage
Toad Heaven
Toad Away
Toad Surprise
Boy Overboard
Girl Underground
Worm Story
Aristotle's Nostril
Doubting Thomas
Give Peas a Chance
Once
Then
Now

GRACE

MORRIS GLEITZMAN

PUFFIN

PUFFIN BOOKS

Published by the Penguin Group
Penguin Books Ltd, 80 Strand, London WC2R 0RL, England
Penguin Group (USA) Inc., 375 Hudson Street, New York, New York 10014, USA
Penguin Group (Canada), 90 Eglinton Avenue East, Suite 700, Toronto, Ontario, Canada M4P 2Y3
(a division of Pearson Penguin Canada Inc.)
Penguin Ireland, 25 St Stephen's Green, Dublin 2, Ireland (a division of Penguin Books Ltd)
Penguin Group (Australia), 250 Camberwell Road, Camberwell, Victoria 3124, Australia
(a division of Pearson Australia Group Pty Ltd)
Penguin Books India Pvt Ltd, 11 Community Centre, Panchsheel Park, New Delhi – 110 017, India
Penguin Group (NZ), 67 Apollo Drive, Rosedale, North Shore 0632, New Zealand
(a division of Pearson New Zealand Ltd)
Penguin Books (South Africa) (Pty) Ltd, 24 Sturdee Avenue, Rosebank, Johannesburg 2196, South Africa

Penguin Books Ltd, Registered Offices: 80 Strand, London WC2R 0RL, England

puffinbooks.com

First published in Australia by Penguin Group (Australia),
a division of Pearson Australia Group Pty Ltd 2009
First published in Great Britain by Puffin Books 2011
1

Text copyright © Creative Input Pty Ltd, 2009
All rights reserved

The moral right of the author has been asserted

Set in Minion
Printed in Great Britain by Clays Ltd, St Ives plc

British Library Cataloguing in Publication Data
A CIP catalogue record for this book is available from the British Library

ISBN: 978-0-141-33603-9

www.greenpenguin.co.uk

Penguin Books is committed to a sustainable future
for our business, our readers and our planet.
The book in your hands is made from paper
certified by the Forest Stewardship Council.

For my parents, Philip and Pamela

Chapter 1

In the beginning there was me and Mum and Dad and the twins.

And good luck was upon us and things were great and talk about happy families, we were bountiful.

But it came to pass that I started doing sins.

And lo, that's when all our problems began.

Chapter 2

At first I didn't know I was a sinner.

I knew I was probably a bit naughty from the way teachers used to look at me and mutter things under their breath. Which was very kind of them. Teachers aren't paid to pray for you, they do it out of the goodness of their hearts.

But nobody ever accused me of having a sinful heart. Not until the day of our backyard barbecue. The one that turned into a disaster, and not just because Mum set fire to her hair and Dad put too much chilli in the sausages.

It was a very important barbecue for our family.

We were celebrating Uncle Vern's big day. Earlier that morning Mum's brother had been made an elder, which was as high up as you could go in our church if you weren't God.

Our backyard was packed. All the other church elders were there, and their families. The sun was shining and friendship was upon us all.

My brothers Mark and Luke were doing a top job of organising games with the other kids. Everyone always said Mark and Luke were the most energetic four-year-old twins in our whole church.

The first game was Daniel In The Lions Den. Mark and Luke were both Daniel. The other kids were the lions. Before they started, Mark reminded the lions how in the Bible story Daniel had mega amounts of faith, so God protected him.

'So no biting,' said Mark to the lions.

'Only waddling,' said Luke.

'Lions don't waddle,' snorted one of the kids.

'It's a lions den and a penguins den,' said Luke.

Soon most of the church elders had taken off their jackets and rolled up their sleeves. Uncle Vern even took off his tie. It was a fun day.

At first.

I was handing round cheesy toast triangles with my friend Delilah. But I could see her mind wasn't on the job. She kept standing on tip-toe and staring over the fence into the neighbours' gardens.

'You are so completely brave living here,' said Delilah.

I knew why she was saying that. My family was a bit different in our church because we didn't have other church members living next door. Our neighbours were all outsiders. Our place was surrounded by the outside world.

'You are so not safe living in this street,' said

Delilah. 'What if an ungodly sinner neighbour wants to borrow your lawnmower?'

If I'd been as completely brave as she reckoned, I would have told her the truth. That we lent it.

But I didn't. Some of the church elders were listening. And they were looking almost as tense as Delilah. Our next-door neighbour Mrs Benotti had just put her washing out and a breeze had sprung up and everybody was keeping away from the fence in case a peg snapped and they got a face full of unbeliever's undies.

'Grace.'

I turned to see who was calling.

It was Grandpop. He was standing near the back door, frowning. I was surprised to see him looking grumpy today. This was meant to be a happy day for him. All morning he'd been getting heaps of congratulations for being Uncle Vern's father. Plus earlier in the week God had spoken to him in person. They had a blessed conversation and God told him the celebration barbecue should be at our place so he and Nannie wouldn't have to worry about their flowerbeds being trampled.

'Grace, come here.'

Grandpop was gesturing impatiently. He'd been a church elder for years and he was used to people doing what he said.

As I hurried over, I saw that Grandpop had somebody with him. Mr Gosper, who was an elder too. Mr Gosper was holding a green folder.

I stared at the folder.

It was my school project.

Confusion came upon me. I'd left the project in my desk drawer in my room. How come Mr Gosper had it?

I realised what must have happened. Mr Gosper must have gone into the house to use the bathroom and afterwards he must have decided to cast an eye around. Church elders often did that when they visited houses to make sure people were obeying church rules. Poor Mr Gosper did it a lot now because he had so much spare time since his wife died.

I wondered if I should whisper to Mr Gosper that the long strands of grey hair he brushed over his bald patch had flopped down over one ear. It's probably what Mrs Gosper would have done.

But Grandpop didn't give me the chance.

'Grace,' he snapped, pointing to my project. 'Did you do this?'

I hesitated. Not because I was planning to commit the sin of lying. Just because sometimes it's hard to get words out when a very tall person is cross with you and you don't know why.

'Yes, Grandpop,' I said quietly. 'It's my school project.'

In church that morning Grandpop had hugged Uncle Vern and announced that this was the happiest and proudest day of his life. He didn't look like it was now.

Mr Gosper was looking pretty annoyed too.

I didn't understand. This project was some of my best work. I'd spent all Saturday doing it. Dad reckoned I had a good chance of getting an A for it, and possibly even a Nobel Prize for Literature.

Suddenly I had a thought.

Perhaps Grandpop and Mr Gosper were cross about my untidy handwriting. Maybe they were annoyed because they couldn't read it.

'May I?' I said.

Politely, I took the folder from Mr Gosper and opened it.

'It's called The Family Bible,' I explained. 'It's like the real Bible except it's about my family and how lucky I am to have them. I've even called the chapters Books like in the real Bible. It's got The Book Of Dad and The Book Of Mum and The Book Of Twins.'

I waited for Grandpop to ask if it had The Book Of Grandpop, which it did. I'd been saving that as a surprise. Grandpop loved the Bible more than any other book in the world.

But Grandpop didn't seem to be feeling the same about my bible.

'Sausage, anyone?' said Dad, stepping between us with a platter of his homemade sausages. 'Lamb and mint or pork and chilli.'

Grandpop gave Dad an angry glare. I wasn't sure if it was because Dad was interrupting, or because he was wearing a Pink Floyd t-shirt when all the other men were wearing their Sunday suits. Or maybe it was because Dad had cooked lunch when in our church only women did that.

'Some of her best work,' said Dad, nodding towards my project. 'Grace, give them a quick reading from The Book Of Mum.'

I hesitated. From the look on Grandpop and Mr Gosper's faces I was starting to think maybe I was wrong about them wanting to read my project.

But Dad gave me a big encouraging smile. Whenever he did that, I always glowed inside. It was like the feeling I got when I said my prayers.

I opened the folder and cleared my throat.

'The Book Of Mum,' I read. 'Chapter four, verse one. And behold, Mum's nineteenth birthday was upon her and that day in church she did look twice at a young bloke and she did like what she saw, and lo, even when his parents moved to America he stayed here and got betrothed to Mum and love came upon them and so did a really nice wedding with cake afterwards at Grandpop and Nannie's place. Verse two. And the bloke's name was Dad and a kind heart was within him and upon his driveway was a Toyota Hilux –'

'Enough,' snapped Grandpop.

I could see he definitely didn't like it.

I glanced at Uncle Vern and the other guests. Nobody seemed to like it, apart from Dad. Some of the other elders were looking like they'd been slapped in the face by one of Mrs Benotti's bras.

7

Mr Gosper shook his head grimly.

'That child,' he said to Dad, 'is mocking the word of our Lord. Look at her, so young and already learning the ways of sin. If I was her father I'd be ashamed of what is happening in her heart.'

'Amen,' muttered Grandpop.

I was shocked. Mr Gosper was known for exaggerating, but Grandpop wasn't. He knew my heart wasn't sinful or bad. Every Saturday we fed the birds in his backyard together.

'I'm sorry, Grandpop,' I said. 'I didn't mean to upset anybody. But I don't get it. Why is it mocking God to write bible things about my family? About their good points and loving habits? I don't think God minds that.'

Grandpop and Mr Gosper were both scowling. I could see they didn't agree. But Dad had taught me to be true to my views.

'Actually I think God likes it,' I said quietly.

'How dare you?' Mr Gosper hissed at me. 'How dare you argue with the Lord's judgement?'

Dad stepped forward and looked Mr Gosper right in the eyes. The heat from the platter of sausages made the air shimmer between them.

'If your heart,' said Dad to Mr Gosper, 'was half as big as Grace's, you'd see what her project is really about. And you'd rejoice instead of making a kid feel small in front of her family and friends.'

I wanted to hug him.

'And insulting her faith,' Dad went on. 'And

destroying her self-confidence. And belittling her handwriting. And crushing her spirit.'

'Actually,' I whispered to Dad. 'It's not quite that bad.'

Mr Gosper put his face even closer to Dad's.

'And what do you think her so-called project is about?' said Mr Gosper.

Dad didn't flinch.

'Same thing as all the best bits of the Bible are about,' he said. 'Same thing as this church of ours should be about.'

Mr Gosper frowned.

'Love,' said Dad.

The screen door banged open and Mum hurried out from the kitchen. Behind her were Nannie and the other women.

Mum stared anxiously at Dad and Mr Gosper, who were still face to face.

'Come on, everybody,' she said. 'Let's eat. Mr Gosper, please, will you say grace for us?'

Mr Gosper didn't even look at Mum. He just kept glaring at Dad, his breath whistling in his nostrils.

Mum gave a cry of alarm. But it wasn't about Dad and Mr Gosper. It was about the next lot of sausages, which had just burst into flames on the barbecue.

Mum leapt across the patio, pulling off her apron and swatting at the flames with it. The violent movements made a couple of her hairpins fall out.

Her bun started to collapse. Wisps of her long hair tumbled down towards the burning sausages.

Suddenly I saw flames climbing up one of the wisps.

People yelled. Mr Gosper called on the Lord's protection. I grabbed a glass of lemonade and threw it over Mum's head.

The burning hair hissed and the flames went out.

'Thanks, love,' said Mum, wiping lemonade out of her eyes. As she pinned her other wisps back up, she muttered to herself.

'Flaming hair.'

I was shocked.

Mum never swore.

But I knew how she felt. There were lots of good things about being in our church, but the rule about women and girls having long hair as a sign of obedience to God was a real pain.

Dad put his arm round Mum.

'Are you OK?' he said gently.

He dabbed her hair with his apron.

Mum nodded and they looked at each other for a moment. I could tell Mum knew that Dad had been standing up for me.

They both turned to the guests, who were all looking a bit stunned.

'Drama's over,' said Mum. She put her arm round Uncle Vern. 'Let's get back to celebrating my big brother's special day.'

'Help yourselves, folks,' said Dad. 'We've got

three types of sausages now. Lamb, pork and charcoal.'

'And penguin,' said Mark, stabbing the air with his plastic sword.

While Mark and the other kids went on a hunt for penguins that might have been mocking the word of our Lord, Luke came over and squinted up at me.

'Mum was on fire,' he said. 'Why was she?'

I explained it was just a little accident and things were OK now.

But for the rest of the afternoon I kept seeing Mr Gosper and Grandpop and Uncle Vern and the other elders talking in groups and throwing looks at me and Dad.

'You are so judged,' Delilah said to me. 'It's cause your Dad put too much chilli in the sausages.'

I beheld that it probably wasn't.

And slowly I started to have a horrible feeling that things weren't OK.

Chapter 3

That night, Mum did a surprising thing.

She suggested me and Dad stay at home and carry on clearing up after the barbecue.

I was a bit stunned. It was Sunday evening. We always went to church on Sunday evening. All of us. Together.

I could see Dad was surprised too.

'Might be best, love,' Mum said to him. 'You saw how the elders were looking at you after your run-in with Mr Gosper. Might be best to make sure they've got over it.'

Dad opened his mouth to argue, then closed it.

Even Dad knew that sometimes other people are probably right.

'Anyway,' said Mum. 'The twins need an early night. And you and Grace can have some time together.'

Dad nodded. I could see he liked the idea. I did too, now I was getting used to it.

But after Mum had gone and we'd put the twins to bed and we were in the kitchen drying the last plates and cups, I was afflicted with an anxious doubt.

'Dad,' I said. 'Do you think the elders will punish Mum because we didn't all go to church?'

Dad thought about this.

'I don't think so,' he said. 'Mum's the daughter of an elder, so they'll be a bit easier on her. Anyway, they'll probably be relieved I'm not there.'

I grinned.

'Yeah,' I said. 'You have been getting into some bulk arguments in church lately.'

Dad looked at me with pretend outrage.

'They're not arguments,' he said, flicking my backside with the tea towel. 'They're discussions. Just people swapping ideas so they can understand God better.'

I didn't say anything.

Dad grinned and wrinkled his nose.

'Alright,' he said. 'Sometimes they're arguments. But only because those dopey elders don't like a person asking perfectly reasonable questions.'

Dad was right about that.

Specially when those perfectly reasonable questions were about the rules of our church. And whether God really wanted the rules to be so strict.

The elders hated those questions the most.

After we finished in the kitchen, me and Dad went into the backyard and lay on the lawn and stared up at the stars and played twenty questions.

In our family we had our own version of twenty questions. It was very simple. Everyone put their minds together and asked the twenty most interesting questions they could think of.

'Dad,' I said, 'this afternoon, when Mr Gosper didn't like my project, why did he say I was arguing with the Lord's judgement? I wasn't, was I?'

That was two questions at the same time, but I knew Dad wouldn't mind.

Dad didn't answer for a while.

It was one of the things I liked about him. When you asked him questions he always gave them a proper think.

'No, Grace,' said Dad after a minute or two. 'You weren't arguing with God. You were arguing with Mr Gosper, which is a very different thing. That's what's wrong with our church these days. Elders who carry on as if they're God.'

I was shocked.

I'd never heard Dad say anything like that before, not even when he was having a big shouting match with the elders. But when I thought about it, I had to admit he was sort of right.

I thought about it for ages, lying there in the backyard staring up at the night sky. Dad didn't say anything else because he knew that's what I was doing.

It was our favourite thing.

Asking questions and thinking about the answers.

After a while I had another one.

'Dad,' I said. 'Do you think I should hand in my project?'

Dad only thought about that for a heartbeat.

'Up to you,' he said.

That was yet another thing I liked about Dad. When he gave you a short answer, he always meant what he said. You didn't have to look for hidden meanings. 'Up to you' meant 'up to you', not 'I think you're crazy if you do because you'll get into trouble and so will our family but I don't want to look like a bossy-boots so I'm pretending I'm giving you the choice.'

Dad gently touched my arm.

'What am I always going on about?' he said.

I knew the answer to that question.

'Being true to myself,' I replied.

'That's right,' he said.

'I am going to hand it in,' I said.

'Good,' said another soft voice in the darkness.

Mum was home. She lay next to us on the grass, and cuddled in close.

'I have a feeling,' said Mum, 'that tomorrow in class Miss Parry will like your project more than Mr Gosper did.'

I gave Mum a hug.

'How was church?' said Dad.

Mum generally didn't rush into answers either. Except to questions like 'Is your hair on fire?'

'I think we're OK,' she said after a bit.

There was another pause.

In the moonlight I saw that Dad was giving Mum a look.

'Except we're not really, are we?' he said.

Mum gave him a look back.

'We're OK if we want to be,' she said quietly.

My mind was dashing around faster than a locust that had lost the rest of its plague. I was trying to work out what Mum and Dad were talking about.

There was a long pause. I tried to see their faces in the dark. I wasn't sure if their voices were being tense or not.

'What I want,' said Dad to Mum, 'is for us to spend some time talking about what we should be talking about.'

'Not here,' said Mum.

Her voice was suddenly very tense.

'What not here?' I asked.

'Nothing,' said Mum. 'Come on, time for bed.'

'Dad?' I said.

'Mum's right,' said Dad. 'It's late. School day tomorrow. You want to be fresh for your Nobel Prize.'

They chased me into the house, threatening to tickle me. I always enjoyed that, but tonight, in a corner of my mind, something didn't feel right.

I'd asked a question.
They hadn't answered it.
That had never happened in our family before.

Chapter 4

The next morning I did another sin, but only because our school minibus crashed into a truck.

We were speeding through the outside world on our way to school, whizzing along Steve Waugh Boulevard near the Breezy Whale carwash.

Our trip each morning was a bit complicated because the minibus had to pick up kids from about three suburbs. Mr Gosper, who usually drove the bus, liked to do the trip as quickly as possible so we didn't have to spend too much time in the outside world.

I was in the back seat with Delilah and her brother Liam. We were showing each other our projects.

'You are so getting a D minus for that, Grace,' said Delilah, shaking her head at my folder.

'My mum and dad think it's good,' I said.

'That's because they're in it,' said Liam.

'You can't write a bible about your family,' said

Delilah. 'That is so not biblical.'

'The Bible's got a lot of families in it,' I said.

My voice must have been quite loud because Mr Gosper turned round in the driver's seat and gave me a look. He must have realised we were talking about my project. I tried to slide the folder back into my school bag.

'I'm serious,' said Delilah. 'You are so going to be judged.'

Suddenly there was a loud screech and the sound of a plastic bumper bar being rent asunder and talk about whiplash, we were all nearly afflicted with snapped necks. Our homework was cast off our knees onto the floor. Some of the kids screamed.

I peered out the window, trying to see what had happened.

Delilah grabbed me.

'Is this it?' she gasped, her eyes huge.

I shook my head.

Delilah always thought the world was ending. The number of times I had to remind her that she'd know when it was the end by the apocalyptic fire everywhere and the smoke from all the burning fat in McDonald's.

I gave Delilah's arm a comforting squeeze like I always did.

'It's OK,' I said gently. 'God doesn't want to gather us to him just yet.'

I unclicked my seatbelt and stood up and peered out the front window and saw what had happened.

We'd crashed into the back of a tow truck at the traffic lights. Luckily God had helped Mr Gosper get his foot on the brake, so there wasn't too much damage, which was a blessing.

'Mr Gosper,' I said. 'Are you alright?'

Mr Gosper was glaring through the windscreen at the tow truck like it was the tow truck's fault. I didn't think it could be because the tow truck was at the traffic lights first, but I didn't say anything.

'Everybody stay in your seats,' said Mr Gosper.

He got out of the minibus and started examining our broken bumper bar.

I saw that the accident had afflicted Mr Gosper's hair. His long grey wisp had flopped off his bald patch and was hanging down over one ear. Apart from that he didn't seem to be hurt, which was a relief.

I couldn't see if the other driver had been as lucky. Nobody was getting out of the tow truck. The big hook on the back was still swinging from the crash. What if the other driver was injured?

Mr Gosper didn't seem to be checking.

I felt awful. I imagined someone crashing into Dad. Or Mum when she was in the car with Mark and Luke. OK, Mum couldn't drive, but I still imagined it and I was filled with compassion.

That's why I did it.

I squeezed past the kids sitting in front of me, undid the child lock on the sliding door of the minibus and got out.

'Grace,' I heard Delilah say. 'Come back. You mustn't.'

She was right. It was the outside world. The people in it were unsaved sinners. But they were still people.

I went over to the tow truck. I wished Dad was with me. He knew first aid and was very good at calming jangled nerves when he wasn't starting arguments.

Then I noticed what was written in big letters on the side of the truck.

DENNY'S SAVAGE.

For a sec I thought it was a warning about the driver. But I looked again and what it actually said was DENNY'S SALVAGE.

I could hear voices coming from the cab of the truck.

'Flaming thing's jammed,' said a man's voice.

'Hurry up, Dad,' said a kid's voice. 'If the cops see us, we'll be in trouble.'

The driver's window was open. I peered in.

Two people in the driver's seat were sharing the same seatbelt. One was a man in overalls with chin stubble and a pony tail. Perched on the man's knees, with his hands on the steering wheel like he'd been doing the driving, was a boy about my age.

The man was trying to undo the seatbelt.

'I should have fixed this mongrel when it first started playing up,' he grumbled.

The boy leaned forward and rummaged around under the dash.

'There's a screwdriver here, Dad,' he said.

'Are you alright?' I said to them.

They both looked at me, startled.

I was a bit startled myself when I saw that the boy's spiky hair had the words *Go Saints* shaved into it. Then I realised what that meant. Dad had explained once how for a lot of people, footy was their religion.

The tow-truck driver grabbed the screwdriver from his son and did something to the seatbelt buckle, which clicked open.

I took a step back as the tow-truck driver opened the door, lifted his son out and climbed out himself.

'We're right, thanks,' he said gruffly. 'But nice of you to ask.'

He peered towards the back of the truck and saw that one of his rear lights was sorely afflicted and in fragments on the road.

'Aw, Jeez,' he muttered.

'We're really sorry we crashed into you,' I said. 'In our church we're all saved, so we're a bit careless on the road sometimes. It's because we know God's protecting us.'

I hoped I'd explained it properly. It was how Dad had explained it to me one time after he'd had an argument with Mr Gosper, who reckoned speed limits were only for sinners.

The tow-truck driver stared at me, then at the minibus, then at Mr Gosper, who was rummaging around inside the glove box.

'That clown shouldn't be driving kiddies,' the tow-truck driver muttered.

'Mr Gosper has to,' I explained. 'God told him to.'

'Is that right?' snorted the tow-truck driver. 'And did God tell him to go around crashing into people?'

I wasn't certain, but it didn't seem likely.

The tow-truck driver went to have a closer look at the broken light. I started to follow him, but his son grabbed my arm. I went rigid with shock. I'd never been touched by an outsider before. I pulled my arm away, then saw that the boy was offering me something.

It was a bar of chocolate. Some of it had already been eaten. The wrapper was crumpled and the chocolate looked a bit fluffy.

'You can have this,' muttered the boy. 'If you don't tell the police.'

I stared at him. I wasn't sure what he meant.

'About me steering the truck,' said the boy. 'Anyway, I wasn't really steering. My dad had his hands on the wheel too. And he was doing the pedals. But you mustn't say anything cos if he gets busted and loses his licence, he won't be able to do his salvage business.'

I stared at the chocolate, not sure what to say. In our church we weren't allowed to eat things outsiders had touched, not without cooking it first. That's why we had so much soup and toast.

The boy was looking at me pleadingly.

'I didn't ask to steer,' he said. 'But my dad wants me to learn things so I'll get on in life.'

The boy had tough hair, but his eyes were gentle and anxious.

'Don't worry,' I said. 'I'm not allowed to have the chocolate, but I won't tell anyone what you did. Anyway, Mr Gosper won't call the police. Our church doesn't like to get involved with outsiders.'

The boy looked relieved and grateful.

'Thanks,' he said.

We looked at each other. I could see he was wondering something.

'Are you Muslim?' he said.

I shook my head.

'Christian,' I said. 'A special type.'

The boy nodded as he thought about this.

'Grace,' yelled Mr Gosper. 'Get back in the bus.'

I turned. Mr Gosper was coming towards us. He looked furious. Wrath and anger were totally upon him. Poor bloke. Dad reckoned Mr Gosper had stomach ulcers but wouldn't admit it in case people thought Satan had given them to him.

'She wasn't doing anything wrong,' said the boy.

'Don't interfere in things you know nothing about,' snapped Mr Gosper.

'Hey,' said the tow-truck driver angrily to Mr Gosper. 'Take it easy.'

Things were turning ugly. I tried to take a leaf from Mum's book and do what I could to smooth things over.

'Outsiders don't know our rules,' I reminded Mr Gosper. 'We can't just crash into people and expect them to know our rules.'

Mr Gosper glared at me. He thrust a piece of paper into the tow-truck driver's hands and pushed me towards the bus.

I wasn't surprised Mr Gosper was angry for I knew what I had done.

I'd touched an outsider. We'd been told millions of times never to do that. You could catch demons. Sin could flow into you like molten burning fat. You could end up defiled.

The other kids were all staring at me as I climbed into the minibus. In the back seat, Liam and Delilah made room for me. A lot of room. As I sat down they made sure they didn't touch any part of me.

I understood why.

'You are so defiled,' said Delilah.

'You're gunna get crucified when Mr Reece hears about this,' said Liam.

I didn't feel defiled. Dad and me chatted with our neighbours all the time. Dad reckoned catching sin and demons from unsaved people was nonsense and there wasn't any scientific evidence for it.

I tried to discuss with Delilah and Liam what had just happened.

'Do you think,' I said, 'if God had wanted to, he could have stopped us crashing into those outsiders?'

Delilah snorted.

'Duh,' she said. 'Of course.'

'So why didn't he?' I said.

'That is so obvious,' said Delilah. 'He's punishing you for your evil school project.'

'Which is totally unfair on the rest of us,' said Liam. 'And the school bus.'

'What if,' I said, 'this was God's way of giving us the chance to make friends with outsiders?'

Delilah and Liam stared at me, horrified. I'd been trying to help Delilah get better at discussions, but it wasn't easy because she got shocked so easily.

'You are so going to be smitten by wrath,' she said.

Mr Gosper revved the minibus and steered around the tow truck and headed towards school.

I looked out the window. The boy was watching us drive away. He gave a little wave. I waved back. He seemed like a nice person. It made me sad to think that most of the people in my church would think he was an ungodly sinner.

I pushed the thought out of my mind.

I knew Delilah and Liam were probably right about Mr Reece the principal. He wouldn't be happy when he heard what I'd done.

The other kids in the bus knew it too. They were peeking over their shoulders and I could see some of them praying for me, which was very kind.

But sometimes even nineteen kids praying on a bus isn't enough. Not when it turns out you're in the biggest trouble of your life.

Chapter 5

Wrath is like anger, only worse.

It makes people's eyes go furious, and their brows darken, and whole nations die of it sometimes. There's a lot of it in the Bible, and there was quite a bit at school that day.

When we arrived we went straight into assembly.

Mr Reece was on the stage, waiting for us to get settled. He was staring at the floor with grimness upon him. I hoped there wasn't anything serious afflicting his family, specially his little grandson who'd been born with a nasty cough. With a bit of luck Mr Reece was just frowning because he was the school principal and he'd heard that one of his pupils had spoken to unsaved people in a tow truck.

'Let us pray,' said Mr Reece.

After all the usual prayers, Mr Reece opened his eyes and looked straight at me.

'O Lord,' he said, 'we shamefully acknowledge a disobedient and disrespectful child among us.'

He beckoned for me to come out the front.

As I stood up, none of the other kids looked. It was a school rule. Don't stare at a sinner. Put your hands in your lap and lower your eyes and pray that the bad person finds the path of goodness.

I could see Delilah's lips moving, but I couldn't tell if she was praying for me or whispering to the person next to her about how defiled I was.

Trembling, my calm nerves forsaking me, I walked to the front of the hall and up onto the stage. I'd never had this experience before. Usually Mr Reece just called me into his office for a talk about obedience and how I didn't have much and how that made God very cross. Which wasn't so bad because inside I usually didn't agree.

Today, though, what was happening felt very different.

Worry was upon me.

Mr Reece made me stand next to him on the stage. He put his hand on my head.

'O Lord, our Judge and Master,' he said in a loud voice. 'We ask You to rid this child of her disobedience. We beg You to teach her respect for You and for this church. We beseech You to cleanse her disrespectful and sullied heart.'

Now bulk worry was upon me.

Dad's first rule was never lie to God. Lying, Dad always said, should never be part of a friendship.

What Mr Reece had just said to God wasn't true. I didn't have a disrespectful heart. I respected God and God knew that. Plus, I wasn't exactly sure what sullied meant, but I was pretty sure I didn't have that either. I needed to warn Mr Reece that he was telling untruths to the Lord.

'Excuse me,' I said to Mr Reece. 'But that isn't quite right.'

Mr Reece opened his eyes and stared down at me. His nose was turning pink with wrath, which wasn't a good sign. Plus he looked a bit stunned.

People didn't often interrupt prayers in assembly.

Well, never actually.

Other people in the hall were looking stunned too. Miss Parry my class teacher. All the other teachers. The students. Everyone actually.

'I don't think I've got a disrespectful and sullied heart,' I said to Mr Reece. 'I don't feel like I have.'

Mr Reece looked like he was choking on something. I hoped he hadn't had a bacon sandwich just before assembly.

I was feeling a bit dizzy myself. But I made myself think of Dad and his calming voice and how brave he was in church whenever the others shouted at him for asking questions.

'I'm sorry to muck up your prayers,' I said to Mr Reece. 'But my dad reckons the truth is the most important thing.'

Mr Reece didn't speak for a few more moments, but I was relieved to see he was breathing again.

Suddenly he grabbed the Bible from the lectern.

'This is the only truth,' he said. 'God's word. The word of the only Father who matters. The word you insist on questioning with your pride and disobedience.'

I tried to explain how that wasn't right either. It felt a bit rude, having a private conversation on stage, so I explained it in a loud voice so everyone in the hall could hear.

'I'm not trying to be disobedient,' I said to Mr Reece. 'I'm just trying to think for myself. My dad reckons we all should.'

Mr Reece scowled.

'Your father is an ungodly man,' he said.

That made me feel sad and upset. Mr Reece was a smart person, but he'd got it totally wrong about Dad.

'Dad reckons it takes more than a bit of independence to make God cross,' I said. 'He reckons God wants us to ask questions. That's why we've got brains. And computers.'

Mr Reece was still glaring at me.

I could see I needed to explain some more.

'Questions help us understand things,' I said. 'Like, why can only people in our church go to heaven?'

I was hoping Mr Reece would be less wrathful when he saw me giving examples like Miss Parry had taught us to do in essays.

'There must be enough room in heaven for more than just the people in our church,' I continued. 'God can make things as big as He likes. Look at outer space . . .'

Before I could finish, Mr Reece dragged me off the stage.

I was disappointed I couldn't finish my question. A few of the kids were looking interested.

Mr Reece marched me out of the hall and down the corridor towards his office.

'Why do you do this, Grace?' he said. 'Why can't you be more like your friend Delilah? For years I used to think your father was the most disobedient student we'd ever had in this school, but you're worse. How much longer do you think we're going to put up with this behaviour?'

I didn't say anything. I could see Mr Reece didn't want an answer. That was the difference between me and him. When I asked a question I always wanted an answer.

Oh well, at least this was more like a normal day. I knew where I was going now.

To the Bible solitary room.

Chapter 6

There was a knock on the door.

I was sitting in the little Bible solitary room, reading verses from the Bible over and over out loud like you had to. For a sec I thought it was Mr Reece coming back to check I was still reading the ones about obedience and respect. Except Mr Reece didn't usually knock. It wasn't that he was rude, just the principal.

The door opened and Miss Parry came in.

Her face was sad and concerned.

'Oh, Grace,' she said.

I could tell she wanted to say more, but I couldn't work out what. She often had that look in class. Sort of worried and caring. Sometimes I wondered if Miss Parry was an angel in teacher's clothing.

'Don't worry, Miss Parry,' I said. 'I'm fine.'

I thought I was. I'd been in Bible solitary heaps of times. The worst that usually happened was I got a sore throat from all the reading.

Miss Parry gave another sigh.

'Whatever happens, Grace,' she said quietly, 'remember that God will always be with you.'

I guessed Miss Parry must have heard bad things about my family bible project. Mr Gosper must have told them to her.

I reached for the folder in my bag so Miss Parry could read it for herself and make up her own mind. But before I could show it to her, she said something I wasn't expecting.

'Probably best if you tidy yourself up a bit,' she said. 'Before the elders get here.'

I stared at her.

The elders?

Was I in that much trouble?

My hair took ages as usual. I undid the whole lot and rolled it back up as tight as I could and stuck all the hairpins back in. I could see Miss Parry wanted to help me, but of course she didn't because you weren't allowed to touch a person who was in Bible solitary.

I gave Miss Parry a grateful smile anyway. She was lucky. Her hair was completely straight and she wore it tied into a knot completely untroubled by the ways of hairpins.

When I'd finished she stared sadly at my bun.

'That looks lovely,' said Miss Parry. 'The elders like tidy hair. When they see yours, I pray their hearts will open to you.'

I didn't ask Miss Parry what the elders were

coming to punish me for. If she'd been allowed to tell me, she would have done.

As Miss Parry left, I gave her another grateful smile for warning me as best she could. But inside bulk worry was upon me. I knew how Daniel must have felt in the lions' den waiting for the lions to arrive.

Well, not exactly. Lions are magnificent and elegant. Our church elders were stern-looking men in business suits, often with dandruff. It wasn't their fault they were stern. It must be a really stressful job, trying to work out what God wants and making everybody do it and punishing people who don't.

While I waited, I thought about tearing up my project and stuffing it into the ventilator grille in the wall.

I decided not to. Mr Gosper had seen it, so there was no point. Plus doing that would look as if I was ashamed of it, which I wasn't.

Instead I had a quick word with God.

'It's OK,' I said. 'This isn't a big deal. Please concentrate on giving Mum and Dad the strength to solve the problem they didn't want to talk about last night, whatever it is. I'll be fine, even if the elders yell and get angry and punish me a lot. Thanks.'

After I'd read out the obedience and respect verses about fifty times more, the door of the Bible solitary room opened again.

I braced myself.

Uncle Vern came in.

I went floppy with relief.

'Hello, Grace,' said Uncle Vern, smiling.

He was carrying a chair. He sat down on it.

'Hello, Uncle Vern,' I said.

Behold, was I pleased to see him. I'd always liked Uncle Vern. He had the same soft dark eyes as Mum. OK, he was an elder now, but still not scary like the others.

'So, Grace,' he said. 'Bible solitary again, eh?'

I nodded.

'Sorry,' I said.

'These things happen,' said Uncle Vern. 'Would you like a drink? Something to eat?'

'No thanks,' I said.

I was feeling a bit hungry and thirsty, but Uncle Vern must have forgotten that eating and drinking were absolutely forbidden in Bible solitary.

'So,' said Uncle Vern, smiling again. 'That dad of yours, eh?'

I nodded again. I wasn't exactly sure what he meant.

'He does put ideas into your head,' said Uncle Vern. 'Your dad.'

Now I understood. Uncle Vern wanted me to show gratitude, which was another thing we often read verses about in Bible solitary.

'Yes,' I said. 'Dad encourages me to think about a lot of things. His brain is amazing. He probably has more interesting thoughts than any other home lighting warehouse manager in Australia.

Plus he's brilliant at explaining things. Like what the Bible really means. How when it says demons it might just mean jealousy or pimples, stuff like that.'

I stopped. Uncle Vern was frowning. I realised I was probably sounding a bit boastful.

'Sorry,' I said.

'That's OK,' said Uncle Vern.

He looked at me for a while.

A sudden worry came upon me that maybe I was getting Dad into trouble.

'Dad didn't give me the idea for the family bible project,' I said. 'I got that on my own.'

Uncle Vern nodded.

'But,' he said, 'your dad gives you other ideas.'

'Yes,' I said, relieved Dad was off the hook. 'Dad encourages me to think about things and ask questions. And I encourage him back.'

This was feeling a bit weird. Uncle Vern knew me and Dad talked about stuff because he'd heard us do it when he came to our place.

'What sort of questions have you been asking lately?' said Uncle Vern.

I should have thought more carefully before I answered. But sitting in that stuffy room, all I could think was that Dad would want me to tell the truth.

God would too.

'Last week,' I said, 'I asked Dad if animals could go to heaven.'

Uncle Vern frowned again.

'Animals,' he said.

'Yes,' I said. 'And insects.'

'Insects,' said Uncle Vern, frowning even more. 'Like slugs?'

'Sort of,' I said. 'And all those little micro-organisms that live inside us and keep us healthy. It wouldn't be fair if they couldn't go to heaven too.'

Uncle Vern sighed. His shoulders slumped a bit. I felt bad. Some people get nauseous when you talk about tiny creatures living inside us. Except Uncle Vern didn't look nauseous. He looked more like someone with a headache.

He asked me lots more questions about the sort of things me and Dad talked about. I gave him truthful answers, including details of a chat I had with Dad in the backyard about the creation of the universe and whether God had really done it in seven actual normal-type days.

'Dad reckons,' I said, 'that even for God, who's the most amazing creative force in existence and who invented things like love and planets and sleep, seven days is a big ask.'

I could see that poor Uncle Vern was feeling the stress of being a new church elder. He was doing lots of sighing and frowning and rubbing his temples. I started to worry that perhaps the micro-organisms inside Uncle Vern's head weren't doing their job properly.

Finally Uncle Vern stood up.

'Thank you, Grace,' he said. 'God appreciates your honesty.'

That was nice of him.

He pointed to the Bible.

'Keep reading,' he said, and went out.

Uncle Vern must have remembered about the ban on food and drink in Bible solitary, because he didn't offer me any more before he left.

Three hours later I was starving and parched and my throat was just a croak. It was lunchtime, and I couldn't understand why Mr Reece or Miss Parry hadn't come to get me.

This was the longest Bible solitary ever.

As well as hungry and thirsty, I was also worried and confused. I kept thinking how Uncle Vern hadn't actually said why he'd come to see me.

Was I in trouble or not?

To calm myself down, I stopped reading about obedience and respect and read some verses about God loving and protecting children.

The Bible's good like that. There's loads of mega-scary stuff and some bits that make you feel sick, but if you know where to look there are other bits that are like cuddles.

Finally I heard voices talking softly in the corridor outside. I could tell one voice was Uncle Vern's and the other was Mr Reece's.

I didn't usually listen to other people's private

conversations, but I was desperate to find out how much longer I'd have to stay in that room.

I pressed my ear to the door. I still couldn't hear much. Just a few words here and there.

'Regrettable' was one.

'Painful decision' were two others.

And 'break it to her'.

I didn't have a clue what Uncle Vern and Mr Reece were talking about. Not until I heard one other word.

'Expelled.'

I went weak with shock. So weak I almost had to sit down again. But I needed to be sure. I pulled the door open.

As soon as they saw me, Uncle Vern and Mr Reece stopped talking. It didn't matter. I could tell from the guilty looks on their faces what had come to pass.

I was being expelled from school.

I gaped at them, stunned.

How could they?

This was the only school our church had. People in our church weren't allowed to go to any other school. If I was expelled I'd have to stay at home. No friends. No teachers. Just Mum and Dad's disappointed faces.

'Please,' I begged Uncle Vern and Mr Reece. 'Don't.'

Uncle Vern grabbed my shoulder and tried to steer me back into the room.

'Grace,' he said. 'You shouldn't be listening.'

'Back inside, young lady,' said Mr Reece sternly. 'You know you mustn't leave the Bible solitary room until you're told to.'

'It won't be much longer,' said Uncle Vern. 'Sit tight and we'll bring you something to eat and drink.'

My head was almost bursting. Heaps of confused questions were upon me.

Was I being cast out because of my project? Or assembly? Or the tow-truck driver's son? I shouldn't have let him touch me. Nobody wants you in their school if they think you're defiled.

'Uncle Vern,' I said, close to tears. 'Is this because I've got demons?'

He didn't reply. Just exchanged a look with Mr Reece.

'I don't think I have got demons,' I said. 'I don't feel like I have.'

Uncle Vern gave a long sigh.

'You haven't,' he said. 'Not any more.'

I didn't understand. But before I could ask Uncle Vern what 'not any more' meant, they pushed me back inside the Bible solitary room.

As the door was closing I turned my head to one side, desperately hoping they'd notice my nice neat bun and have second thoughts about chucking me out. Then I realised that after three and a half hours, I probably had wisps out everywhere.

The door closed.

I slumped down in the chair.

I asked God not to let it happen.

'Please don't let them expel me,' I said.

But even as I was asking, I knew I shouldn't be doing that.

The first thing Dad ever taught me about God was don't expect Him to do miracles every time you've got a problem. Ask for His advice, yes. Ask for His encouragement, OK. But we have to solve our problems ourselves. If we need help making something happen, or stopping something, that's what families and friends are for.

'Sorry,' I said to God. 'I forgot.'

I listened at the door.

When I was sure Uncle Vern and Mr Reece had gone, I walked quickly and quietly out of the Bible solitary room and out of the school and went to get Dad's help.

Chapter 7

I sprinted through the outside world to the home-lighting warehouse where Dad worked.

The warehouse was in a completely different suburb to the school. It was a long sprint, specially with a heavy school bag and an anxious heart.

I was lucky I wasn't killed.

I forsook pedestrian crossings and just dashed between moving cars without even thanking them. For there was a nagging fear inside me that if I didn't get to Dad in time it would be too late. Once me being expelled was official, I might never be able to get back in. Not even if Dad used his best arguments and I promised to be meek and obedient for ever more.

I did stop outside a phone box with the idea of ringing Dad. Public phones were forbidden in our church because outsiders used them, but this was an emergency.

Then I remembered I didn't have money on me,

or Dad's phone number, plus I wasn't even sure how phone boxes worked.

So I sprinted on, wishing we didn't have the other church rule about phones. The one that said you couldn't have a mobile until you were twenty-one in case you were tempted to visit ungodly websites or ring outsiders for social purposes.

Which made me even more anxious.

Because if I got expelled, what would I be able to do all day except visit websites?

At last I arrived at Dad's work.

When I was a little kid, I used to think heaven would be just like the home-lighting warehouse. Huge and air-conditioned, with soft music playing non-stop and thousands of pretty lights hanging from the ceiling.

I used to love being there. The staff were kind and friendly, even the ones I'd never sat next to at church.

It was a happy place.

The day woe came upon our family, it was very different.

I ran panting into the warehouse and behold, nobody would talk to me.

Not a single person.

'Hi, Samuel,' I said to a nice man with freckles who was Delilah's cousin. 'Have you seen my dad around?'

It was like Samuel didn't even hear me. He

pretended to look closely at something on the cash register screen. But I could see there weren't even any numbers on it.

Had he heard about me being expelled?

Was this how much disgrace I was in?

I ran from one end of the warehouse to the other, asking every staff member I saw if they knew where Dad was, and talk about rude, not one of them answered. They all just looked away.

I was tempted to start asking customers, even though the church rule was you could only speak to outsiders if you were selling them something. But most of the customers wouldn't even have known who Dad was.

'Mr Olsen,' I pleaded. 'Do you know where my dad is?'

Mr Olsen was the assistant manager. He knew where everything was, even screw-in bulbs for old-fashioned Christmas lights. But he did the same as the others. Stared at me with a very uncomfortable look on his face, then pretended to be busy with some lava lamps.

An unchristian temper came upon me, that's how stressed I was.

Poo to you all, I thought. I'll find him myself.

I raced to the back of the store and up the metal stairs to Dad's office. He wasn't often in it, because he liked to work down with the other staff. But it was the only other place I could think of.

Dad wasn't in his office now.

Neither was anything else much.

Dad's office was bare. No books on his shelves, no clutter on his desk. Even the framed photo of me and Mum and the twins that we'd given him for his birthday wasn't on the wall.

Everything was in cardboard boxes on the floor.

I stared at the boxes, my brain darting around like a plague of locusts having an anxiety attack.

Fear was upon me that something terrible had happened. Something even worse than me being expelled.

If a person's had an accident, I thought frantically to myself, and he's at the hospital or the police station or the smash repair shop, you don't bung his belongings into boxes. You only do that if he's not coming back.

And then I had a very scary thought.

It made me feel sick.

'Please,' I said to God, 'don't rapture my dad.'

Dad and me had talked about rapture. Whether it ever really happened. Whether God ever snatched a faithful person to him in a blink so they just disappeared from earth. We didn't think so. Some people in our church believed it, but we'd never heard of it happening. Grandpop reckoned it would only happen after the end of the world. Anyway, one thing Dad was definitely sure of. God wouldn't break up families.

I agreed with him.

'Sorry,' I said to God. 'Just panicking.'

I tried to picture God nodding in an understanding way. Sometimes just seeing him in my imagination was enough to calm me down.

I felt a bit calmer now, but I still wanted to take all the things out of the boxes and put them back where they belonged.

Before I could, I suddenly heard something. Footsteps clanging behind me.

I turned round.

It was my cousins, Cain and Turk, hurrying up the stairs.

'Hello, Grace,' said Cain, with a fake friendly smile. 'Our dad thought we'd find you here.'

'He told us to give you a lift home,' said Turk. 'He said we can buy you a slushy on the way.'

I thought about running. But I knew I'd never be able to push past them on the narrow stairs. For Cain and Turk both did body-building and they were so big and muscly they almost didn't fit into their carpet-warehouse uniforms.

'Where's my dad?' I said.

I was pretty sure they must know. Their dad was Uncle Vern who owned the home-lighting warehouse as well as the carpet warehouse next door.

Cain and Turk gave each other a look, but didn't say anything.

They carried on not saying anything as they led me down the stairs and towards the exit. I could see hesitation was upon them. They wouldn't even look at me.

'Where's my dad?' I asked again, several times.

Cain and Turk kept glancing at each other nervously.

It was almost like they were scared to answer me.

I didn't get it.

Why would two big tough twenty-three year-olds be scared to answer a kid?

Finally Cain spoke.

'That's real rough about your father being fired,' he said.

I stared at him.

Fired?

'We only heard about it this morning,' said Turk. 'Our dad sent us over here earlier to collect your dad's company car and mobile.'

I felt dizzy with confusion.

And a bit of relief.

At least Dad wasn't injured. Fired wasn't so bad. People said sorry and got their old jobs back all the time. Except why had Dad been fired? He was a brilliant home lighting warehouse manager. Uncle Vern was always saying that.

'What flavour slushy do you like?' said Cain.

'Where's my dad now?' I said.

Cain and Turk looked away again. I could see they didn't want to tell me.

'Where?' I yelled.

The staff weren't ignoring me now. They were ignoring the customers and staring at me.

I didn't care.

'Tell me,' I yelled again.

'They took him away,' said Turk.

'Took him away?' I said. 'Who?'

Cain and Turk looked at each other. They didn't want to say. I could see they'd rather be somewhere else. In the gym probably.

'Who?' I yelled.

A group of customers moved away from us.

'The security company we use,' muttered Cain.

I stared at him.

'It's what happens when somebody gets expelled,' mumbled Turk.

This was crazy. It didn't make sense.

'I don't understand,' I said to them. 'Why would my dad get fired and taken away by a security company just because I've been expelled?'

Cain and Turk looked confused.

'You haven't been expelled,' said Cain. 'Your dad has.'

They started marching me towards the exit more quickly. I let them do it because now mega-confusion was upon me.

Dad couldn't be expelled. He left school years ago.

Then I realised what Cain meant and talk about the end of the world, I felt like I'd been whacked by a thunderbolt of woe.

Panic blocked my throat and I needed God's help to breathe. I completely lost the strength in my legs. I would have collapsed on the floor if Cain and Turk hadn't been holding my arms.

I squeezed my eyes shut, trying to block out the fierce burning lights and my tears.

What Cain meant was that Dad had been expelled from the church and from the sight of God.

And in our church, when somebody got expelled, their family never saw them again.

Chapter 8

'Good slushy?' said Turk as Cain steered the car into my street.

I didn't know.

I didn't care.

I sat in the back of the big four-wheel drive, holding the drink container they'd put into my hands. It was cold. My hands were numb.

So was the rest of me.

I just wanted to get home and see Mum and Grandpop. And find a way of getting Dad back.

I had faith we could do it. I knew Dad wouldn't have been thrown out of the church just for having too many arguments. He'd been doing that for years. My project must have had something to do with it. And me talking to outsiders. And me interrupting school prayers. And me leaving the Bible solitary room without permission.

In our church, fathers were meant to be strict and make their families be meek and obedient. If families did sins, fathers got the blame.

So it was up to me.

I knew what I had to do.

Explain to the church elders it was my fault. Beg them to forgive me. Promise to be meek and obedient for the rest of my life.

I had faith I could do that too.

As soon as Cain parked in our driveway, I left the slushy on the back seat and got out.

Cain and Turk got out as well.

'Our dad said we have to take you to Grandpop,' said Turk.

Grandpop's car was also parked in our driveway. This was good. Grandpop was a church elder. He sat in the front row in church. He knew the first names of all the other elders. He must be able to do something.

Organise an afternoon tea, for example, where I could say sorry and promise never to do anything bad ever again, including in school projects.

Perhaps he could organise it today.

'Come on,' I said to Cain and Turk. 'Round the back.'

I knew that everyone would probably be in the kitchen. In our church the women mostly stayed at home in the kitchen in case somebody got hungry. And the men spent a lot of time there eating.

Unless they were Dad, who spent a lot of time there cooking.

I took a deep breath. Until Dad was back, I had to be careful. If I thought about him too much I'd get upset. And I wouldn't be able to help Mum and Grandpop get him back if I was blubbing.

As we came through the carport, I heard my brothers playing in the backyard. It was Mark and Luke's favourite place. First thing in the morning till bedtime prayers they were out there, smiting unbelievers and Philistines with their plastic swords.

They spotted us and stopped playing. They dropped their swords and came over. I beheld frowns on their sweaty little foreheads.

'God made Mummy cry,' said Mark.

'She wasn't naughty,' said Luke. 'Why did God?'

I gave them both a hug and reminded them that God is kind and doesn't make people cry even when they have been naughty.

'Don't worry,' I said to them. 'Play nicely and I'll cheer Mum up.'

Mark and Luke looked at me doubtfully.

I could see what they were thinking. You're a girl. You haven't even got a sword. What can you do?

That was one problem with the Bible. The action heroes were all men. Dad was always saying that.

'Cain and Turk will help me cheer Mum up,' I said. 'Won't you, Cain and Turk?'

Cain and Turk looked doubtful, but nodded. Under their big muscles and tightly stretched carpet-warehouse uniforms my cousins had good hearts.

The twins' faces brightened. They picked up their weapons.

'I'm the good Samaritan,' yelled Mark.

'I'm the bad Samaritan,' yelled Luke, swinging his sword at Mark's head.

I turned and went into the house.

As I came into the kitchen, Nannie looked up from the stove and when she saw me her eyes went soft with concern, just like Mum's often did.

She came over and grabbed my hands.

'Oh, Grace,' she said tearfully. 'You poor child.'

For a moment tears were almost upon me too. Nannie was the most warm-hearted and loving grandmother in the world, but she did cry heaps. I didn't blame her. Grandpop could be pretty strict.

'Where's Mum?' I asked.

'She's resting in her room, love,' said Nannie. 'She needs some time on her own.'

Part of me wanted to go straight to Mum and comfort her. But that wouldn't get Dad back.

Grandpop was sitting at the kitchen table waiting for his meal.

I took a deep breath.

'Grandpop,' I said. 'There's been a terrible mistake. Dad's been expelled and taken away by a security company. The church elders must think Dad doesn't love God and he does.'

I looked at Grandpop pleadingly.

Grandpop didn't say anything. He just stared at the table.

'I know it's mostly my fault,' I said. 'And I want to say sorry. About my project and all the other things. To you and Mr Gosper and Mr Reece and Uncle Vern and the other church elders. So Dad can come home.'

Grandpop stood up.

He touched the sides of my face gently with his big hands. Hope was within me. He'd never done that before. Then he gripped my shoulders and closed his eyes. I'd never seen him look so sad.

'O Lord,' he said. 'Help this child accept Your will. Help her understand why this family is being punished. Help her bear the pain that we all must bear.'

I didn't understand.

Why was Grandpop saying this?

Tears were stinging my eyes. I wished Dad was there with his arms round me. One of his corny jokes would have been bountiful right then.

Grandpop opened his eyes and looked at me.

'We begged your father to obey the laws of our church,' he said sadly. 'To be obedient. To stop questioning everything. But he wouldn't. So we had to send him away to save you from his dark and sinful heart.'

I stared at Grandpop.

Shock was upon me.

I opened my mouth to tell him that Dad had a warm and faithful and loving heart. Before I could speak Grandpop put his fingers over my mouth.

'Hush, innocent child,' he said. 'When you're older you'll understand.'

I pushed his hand off my mouth.

'No I won't,' I said. 'Because it's not fair. Dad hasn't got a dark and sinful heart, he's just got a lively mind. Which God gave him.'

The kitchen went very quiet except for something bubbling on the stove.

Grandpop took his other hand off my shoulder. Cain and Turk took a step back. I could see they were scared that Grandpop would boil over, which he did sometimes.

I didn't care.

Nannie hurried over with a bowl of soup for Grandpop. He ignored it. Nannie gave me a damp hug.

'The security people didn't hurt your dad,' she said. 'They took him to a hotel.'

'A four-star one,' said Cain. 'All expenses paid for the night.'

'Room service,' said Turk. 'In-house movies.'

Cain and Turk were sounding like they wouldn't mind being expelled from church themselves. Until Grandpop gave them a look.

Nannie went back to the stove.

Grandpop turned to me. His face was still sad, but very stern.

'I know this is hard for you, Grace,' he said. 'You're a child and you must do something no child should ever have to do. You must forget you had a father.'

I stared at him in stunned horror.

'God is your Father now,' said Grandpop. 'God will help you to be strong.'

The others all nodded. Nannie sniffed tearfully.

I stared at them, speechless.

I wanted to ask Grandpop how he would like it if Mum, who was his daughter, forgot she had a father. But I didn't because I realised what was happening. Poor Grandpop and Nannie and the others were scared to stand up for Dad in case the church elders thought they were being disobedient and expelled them too.

'Would you like some broccoli and cheese soup?' said Nannie.

I didn't blame them. The elders could be very strict. Even to other elders. But luckily Dad had me and Mum to stand up for him.

I heard faint wailing. For a sec I thought it was Mum. But it was just Mark and Luke smiting each other in the backyard.

I took some deep breaths. At least Grandpop was right about one thing. I did feel God helping me to be strong.

'Dad'll be back,' I said to them. 'He won't stay in some dumb hotel room being cast out. He'll come back and sort all this out and Mum will help him.'

Grandpop gave a big sigh.

'You poor child,' he said. 'Try to understand. He's gone. You won't see him again.'

My head felt like it was a bit of Jericho exploding.

Nannie, who was still crying, came over and grabbed my hands again.

'God gives,' she sobbed, 'but He also takes away.'

'When sins have been committed, He takes away,' said Grandpop.

I didn't believe them.

'God wouldn't take my dad away,' I said.

I twisted and wriggled and finally broke free from Nannie. She said something in a pleading voice. Grandpop spoke very sternly at me. I ignored them both.

I ran out of the kitchen to find Mum.

Chapter 9

Mum was in her room, sitting on the edge of the bed, her head bowed.

She was holding her Bible. Her tiny Bible covered in soft blue leather that Dad gave her when they got married.

I stopped in the doorway.

I didn't want to interrupt Mum's prayers. But she looked up and saw me. Her sad face went surprised.

'You're home from school early,' she said.

I could tell from her voice she wasn't sure if I knew about Dad.

I told her everything. The minibus crash. The *Go Saints* kid. How I made Mr Reece's nose go pink in assembly. How I left the Bible solitary room without permission. How I thought I was expelled.

How I discovered it was actually Dad who was expelled instead.

'It's my fault,' I said. 'I know Dad gets into trouble

in church quite a bit, but I'm the straw that broke the elders' backs.'

'Oh, love,' said Mum.

She put her arms round me and hugged me tight.

'I want to repent,' I said. 'I want to show them I can be meek and obedient. But Grandpop won't listen or organise an afternoon tea or anything.'

'Grace,' said Mum. 'I want you to listen to me. None of this is your fault.'

I looked at her.

How could it not be my fault?

'I mean it,' said Mum. 'It's not.'

I beheld from her face that she meant it. And I knew I could trust her to tell me the truth.

'Then why has Dad been expelled?' I said.

Mum stared down at her Bible. She sighed and I saw how wet her face was.

'I begged him,' she said quietly. 'I begged him so many times not to get into arguments at church. Yes, the rules are too strict sometimes. Yes, the elders can be pig-headed. But the price we pay for all the wonderful things our church gives us is that we have to keep our thoughts to ourselves.'

Mum touched my face. I think she was checking for tears but I didn't have any. God was still helping me be strong.

I didn't say anything. My mind was busier than a gang of slaves building a pyramid.

I beheld what Mum was saying. God wanted

us to think for ourselves, but that didn't mean He wanted us to go around asking questions that upset elders. Not as often as Dad did. Not so often that the elders couldn't stand it any more and chucked you out.

'Don't worry,' I said to Mum. 'Dad'll realise he's gone too far. He'll come back and apologise and they'll have to let him back in.'

Mum nodded, but she didn't say anything. I understood. There's only so much grief and worry a person can take before they temporarily lose the power of speech. You see it in the Bible all the time.

I put my arms round her.

'Dad'll be back,' I said softly, and lo, I was right.

I must have fallen asleep, because when I heard Dad's voice it was in my dream. Then I woke up and I was in my own bed, in darkness, and Dad's voice was coming from outside, down in the street.

I scrambled to the window.

Dad was standing in the circle of light from a street lamp.

'I want to see my family,' he was saying loudly. 'This is Australia, not fourth-century Egypt. Let me see my family.'

People were blocking his way. Uncle Vern and Cain and Turk. Plus two other men who worked in the carpet warehouse.

'Show me one place in the Bible,' Dad said to

them, 'where it says a bloke can't see his family.'

The carpet warehouse men tried to grab Dad. He pushed them away.

I slid the window open wider.

'Dad,' I yelled.

He looked up and saw me.

'Don't worry, Grace,' he said. 'It'll be OK.'

While he was looking up at me, he took his eyes off the others and Turk grabbed him in a bear hug. The carpet warehouse men grabbed him too, and started pushing him down the street.

'Let him go,' I yelled.

They ignored me.

I tried to calm everyone down and remind them they were Christians.

'*Behold,*' I shouted at the men in the street. '*For God is not the author of confusion, but of peace.*'

It always worked when Miss Parry said it in class. But the warehouse men mustn't have been fans of that bit in the Bible because they ignored it too. They kept pushing Dad and only stopped when Mrs Benotti from next door came out and threatened to call the police.

I rushed downstairs, thanking God for giving us such a kind neighbour.

But when I reached the street, Mrs Benotti had gone indoors and the warehouse men were grabbing Dad again.

'Stop that,' I shouted.

I tried to get closer to Dad, but I was grabbed

too. Cain got his arm around my chest and I was like a bundle of chaff.

'This is my house, you mongrels,' Dad shouted. 'I've got a right to see my family.'

'You know you can't, Gavin,' said Uncle Vern. 'You've been expelled.'

Dad stared at Uncle Vern with the expression he always got when an argument was starting.

'Why can't we just discuss this?' said Dad. 'Or is discussing things against the law now? Is there an Anti-Theological-Disputation Act I've missed?'

I silently begged Dad not to use long words. Things always got worse when he used them.

'You know why you've been expelled,' said Uncle Vern in his church elder voice.

'I just want to see my wife,' shouted Dad, struggling.

'She doesn't want to see you,' said Uncle Vern.

I was shocked to hear my own uncle tell such an evil lie.

Well that's what I thought. Until Uncle Vern held his mobile out to Dad, and Dad put it to his ear.

'Deb?' he said.

He listened for a while, and then his shoulders slumped and he handed the phone back.

'See?' said Uncle Vern.

Talk about gobsmacked.

I was.

Totally.

I couldn't believe it. Mum would never say she

didn't want to see Dad. There must be a mistake.

Cain was still gripping me tight but I managed to peer around to try to see where Mum was. There was no sign of her running out of the house to explain that it was all a misunderstanding.

The warehouse men were leading Dad to a parked car.

'No,' I screamed.

Dad said something to them. They both looked at me. Then they brought Dad over.

Cain let go of me.

'There's been a mistake,' I said to Dad. 'That couldn't have been Mum on the phone. It must have been somebody putting on a voice.'

Dad gave me a long hug.

'It's OK, love,' he whispered. 'God will give us the strength to find a way through this. Be strong, and help Mum be strong too.'

The warehouse men pulled Dad away from me.

I didn't understand.

Why couldn't Dad tell it was someone putting on a voice?

'I'll see you clowns in court,' Dad said to Uncle Vern and the other men. 'Give you a chance to get acquainted with a couple of the Lord's more popular inventions. Reason and justice.'

The warehouse men put Dad in the car and drove off with him.

Cain didn't try to grab me again. He could see I wasn't moving because woe and confusion were upon me and I was having a lot of trouble being strong.

'Are you OK?' he asked.

I ignored him.

Uncle Vern came over.

'You poor kid,' he said. 'You shouldn't have to go through that. Why couldn't he just do what he was told and stay away?'

I could see Uncle Vern didn't want an answer, so I ignored him too and hurried indoors.

There was a question I desperately wanted an answer to.

What was going on?

Chapter 10

I ran into the lounge room.

Mum was sitting on the settee. Her face was pale and she was holding her Bible so tightly her knuckles were white.

'They've taken Dad away,' I said. 'There's been a mistake. Dad thinks you don't want to see him.'

I felt bad even saying it. Mum obviously knew there'd been a mistake, that's why she was looking so miserable. But why hadn't she come outside to explain?

'There hasn't been a mistake,' said Grandpop's voice.

I turned round.

Grandpop was standing just inside the doorway with his arms folded.

'There hasn't, has there,' he said to Mum.

It wasn't a question.

Mum didn't say anything. Didn't tell Grandpop he was totally wrong. Didn't tell me everything was going to be OK. Just chewed her lip and kept her hands clenched as if a mega-struggle was going on within her.

I couldn't believe what was happening.

I sat next to her.

'Mum?' I said, pleading.

Nannie hurried in and gave Mum a cup of tea. Mum held it as if she didn't even know it was in her hands.

'We have to go and get Dad back,' I said to Mum. 'Or at least try to phone him.'

Mum looked at me. She tried to say something. But she had so much misery upon her she couldn't get the words out.

Grandpop came and stood over us.

'No, Grace,' he said. 'We won't be doing any of that.'

I stared at him. I stared at Mum. I stared back at Grandpop.

Nobody was saying anything.

Nannie started to cry.

'Mum,' I pleaded. 'Tell Grandpop. Tell him you want Dad to come back.'

Mum's eyes filled with tears.

'Oh, Grace,' she said. 'I do want Dad to come back, but it's not that simple.'

Grandpop sat next to me on the settee. I wanted to get up and run, but the room had gone wobbly and I was having trouble breathing, so I stayed there.

'A clever girl like you,' Grandpop said to me, 'probably knows how many humans there are on earth.'

'About six billion,' I said numbly.

'And of those six thousand million souls,' said Grandpop, 'how many will go to heaven?'

I stared at him.

Cataclysmic woe was upon our family and he wanted to do a Sunday school quiz?

'Eleven thousand four hundred and twenty-two,' said Grandpop. 'That's how many members of our church there are around the world. Less than twelve thousand of us have been chosen by the Lord to dwell with Him. And until that time comes, all God requires is that we obey the rules. Including the one that forbids us to live with outsiders.'

Grandpop was a very important man, but I wasn't going to let him get away with that.

'My dad is not an outsider,' I shouted. 'So you're wrong. There are eleven thousand four hundred and twenty-three of us.'

I sat in front of my bedroom mirror, miserably brushing my hair.

In our church, if you were female, the longer your hair got, the more devout and obedient the elders thought you were. And they told us how each night when we brushed our hair, we were making our faith stronger.

Tonight my hair was tangled and I couldn't even

get the brush all the way through it.

I put my hairbrush down and closed my eyes.

Grandpop and the other elders must have told Mum it was a sin to want Dad back. If she believed them, what could I do?

I sat with my face in my hands and for the first time in my life hopelessness was upon me.

But only for a moment.

Then I felt the hairbrush moving through my hair in strong, gentle strokes. I looked up. It was Mum. She was standing behind me, brushing out the tangles. She must have come in while I was being depressed.

'There's something I haven't told you, love,' said Mum quietly. 'The main reason Dad's been expelled. I didn't want to worry you, but I can see now you need to know.'

Mum hesitated and I could see that painful thoughts were upon her.

She was right, I did need to know.

'Tell me,' I said.

Mum took a deep breath.

'Last week,' she said, 'Dad mentioned something in church he shouldn't have.'

Mum hesitated again.

'What was it?' I said.

'For the last few months,' she said, 'Dad's been trying to persuade me to leave the church. With you and the twins. He wants us all to leave the church together.'

I stared at her, shocked.

'I know,' said Mum. 'But poor Dad's been in torment for a long time. He's been getting more and more unhappy. He says the church tries to control our lives too much. How we think. And he doesn't reckon it's fair on you kids.'

I struggled to take all this in.

I could see Dad's point. But it wasn't that bad. He and Mum had taught me to think for myself and they'd do that for Mark and Luke too. OK, from now on we'd have to keep our thoughts to ourselves a bit more, but we could manage that.

Poor Dad. I knew he was trying to do his best for us all, but he didn't have to go this far. God would be so hurt if we left the church. Plus we'd never be allowed to see our family and friends again.

I looked at Mum anxiously.

'What about you?' I said. 'You don't want to leave the church, do you?'

Mum hesitated, but only for a second.

'Our family has been in this church for three generations,' she said.

I could tell from her voice how she felt. She didn't think we should leave the church either.

I should have felt relieved, but I didn't. Because now I beheld how bad things were. How hard it would be to get Dad back.

'Is this the reason?' I said. 'Why you didn't want to see Dad tonight?'

Mum put the hairbrush down.

'Try to understand, love,' she said. 'The church needs to punish Dad and I have to go along with that.'

I opened my mouth to tell her she didn't, but Mum gently put her fingers on my lips.

'It's for Dad's sake,' she said. 'If we let the elders do their punishment, there's a better chance they'll let Dad back in later. And I want that as much as you do, Grace.'

I thought about this.

Then I put my arms round Mum's waist and hugged her.

How could I ever have doubted her?

Instead of getting depressed, I should have been thinking of ways I could help get Dad back.

Chapter 11

In bed I talked to God for a long time.

I told Him I forgave Grandpop for his mean maths, because I knew poor Grandpop was just scared that having Dad around would stop us all getting into heaven.

'As if,' I said to God.

I told Him Mum didn't need to be forgiven, because she was doing what she thought was best for Dad. And because Grandpop had been a really strict father when she was little. I knew God would understand how hard it is to stand up to a parent you're scared of, even though like me He'd never actually had the experience himself.

'We're lucky,' I said to God.

I thanked Him for helping me work out a way of getting Dad back. It was a simple plan. I was going to find Dad and beg him to stop getting into arguments in church and persuade him to be meek and obedient so the elders would allow him back in.

'Thanks heaps,' I said to God.

Finally I told God I was going to do my best to be meek and obedient myself in future so our family would never be in trouble with the elders again. But first I was going to have to break a few church rules to find Dad and for that I apologised in advance.

'Sorry,' I said to God. 'I hope you understand.'

It was very late when I finished talking to God.

But I still had lots to do.

I reached under my bed and slid out the cordless phone I'd hidden there. I took the phone book from under my pillow, pulled the covers over my head, and dialled.

Finding Dad wasn't as simple as I'd hoped.

When you start ringing all the hotels in the phone book at 2am in a kid's voice and asking them if they're four star, a lot of them won't tell you. And even the nice ones get a bit grumpy when you ask for a person who's not even staying there.

'Gavin Hillgrove,' I whispered to yet another hotel.

'You'll have to speak up,' said the cross voice at the other end.

Before I could explain that I had to keep my voice low on account of the large number of people sleeping on camp beds at our place tonight, the covers were pulled off me and the phone was snatched from my hand.

I blinked in the glare from my bedside lamp.

Uncle Vern was standing there with the phone to his ear.

'It's the Hilton,' I said.

Uncle Vern hung up.

'So, Grace,' he said. 'Would you like a drink? Something to eat?'

'It's the middle of the night,' I said.

Uncle Vern nodded for a while.

'You're going to be a much happier girl,' he said, 'if you can manage to do one very difficult thing. Pretend your dad's dead. I know it's painful. I feel terribly sad too. We'll all be grieving for a long time. But it's what we have to do.'

I thought about this.

'He's not dead,' I said.

Uncle Vern frowned. I hoped he wasn't getting another headache.

'OK,' he said gently. 'Think of it like this. Your dad's a plane that has tragically crashed. The plane is lost. It can't be found. It's gone.'

I didn't say anything.

Uncle Vern stood looking at me for a while.

'Any time you need to talk to me, you can,' he said.

'Thanks,' I said.

He turned off the light and went out with the phone.

I lay awake, thinking.

Uncle Vern was wrong. Dad wasn't lost. He just needed to be found.

Next day at school I asked Delilah to help me.

'Ring up hotels?' said Delilah, horrified. 'In the outside world? I so can't do that. Unsaved sinners sleep in those places. Other ones answer the phones. That is so unfair of you to ask.'

'Just a few,' I begged. 'I can't ring them all myself. It'll take too long.'

Delilah made me sit down in a quiet corner of the lunch room. She put her arm round me.

'I'm mega-sad for you about your dad,' she said. 'I mean you must so deserve it in God's eyes, but I'm still sad for you.'

'Thanks,' I said.

With Delilah it was best to appreciate the good bits and ignore the rest.

'I want you to know,' said Delilah, 'that my dad is always available for a lend. You know, for birthday parties and leaking roofs and stuff.'

'Thanks,' I said again.

She really was a good friend.

'I appreciate the offer,' I said, 'but I won't need your dad, because I've got one of my own.'

Delilah rolled her eyes.

'Grace,' she said. 'I'm serious, you are so going to be judged if you carry on like this.'

Miss Parry wished she could help.

'From the bottom of my heart, Grace,' she said as we sat in a quiet corner of the staff room.

I could see she did.

I could also see something was stopping her.

'I'd lose my job,' she said quietly. 'If the elders caught me going against their wishes, I'd be expelled like your poor father.'

Miss Parry looked so miserable I wanted to give her a hug. I hesitated in case there was a rule against it. Then I hugged her anyway. I'd already apologised to God for any rules I broke.

Miss Parry hugged me back.

'Dear Grace,' she said. 'I pray you get the strength you need and the happiness you deserve.'

'Thanks, Miss Parry,' I said.

She glanced around to make sure we couldn't be heard.

'Also,' she said, 'there's not much point ringing hotels now. If your dad was just booked in for one night, he'll have moved on.'

I hadn't thought of that.

I sighed.

I needed help, but I didn't know who else to ask. It was all very well relying on your family for help, but what could you do if they were the thing you needed help with?

'Uncle Vern reckons Dad is a crashed plane,' I said to Miss Parry. 'Lost forever.'

'Not necessarily lost forever,' said Miss Parry. 'They often find crashed planes. It's just that they're hard to salvage.'

I stared at her.

That word she'd just used. Salvage. I'd seen that

word somewhere. I tried to think exactly where. I urgently needed to know, because suddenly I was determined to prove Uncle Vern wrong.

Dad wasn't a crashed plane.

There was hope of salvage.

It took a while, but finally I remembered.

Chapter 12

I'd never been on a train before and talk about stressed, my guts felt more mangled than those two fish Jesus fed five thousand people with.

But as we clattered along the tracks through suburbs I'd never even heard of, I felt very grateful to be there.

Silently I thanked God for the encouragement. I did the same to Miss Parry, who'd been so kind and had explained how trains worked.

'It's for a project, right?' she'd said, and had gone straight on with details of the ticketing system and platform signs before I had a chance to commit the sin of lying.

'Be brave,' she said as I left.

Now, jammed in a train carriage, I knew why.

Rush-hour travel was terrifying. I'd never been squashed up close to outsiders before.

Their rude magazines were quite interesting, but their mouths were full of swear words and greasy breakfasts were upon them.

I reminded myself they were people just like me. Some of them looked almost as stressed as I was. I wondered if any of them had snuck out of the house at 6am to try and salvage their dads and were worrying about what their Mum and Nannie and Grandpop would say.

Probably not.

'Cheer up, love,' said a big man with a shopping bag and a bumpy chin. He winked at me. 'It's not the end of the world.'

I hoped he was right.

And things did improve.

The more stations we stopped at, the more people got off, and after a while I could actually get to my school backpack and pull out the address of Denny's Salvage.

In class once Mr Reece told us about the city of Gomorrah. God decided it was a very sinful place so He smote it and made it fall in a heap, leaving just piles of rubble and junk.

Denny's Salvage depot yard looked like that, but with more old cars.

And a red tow truck.

I stood at the big wire gates and looked at the piles of second-hand bricks and tangled rusting metal and wondered if Mr Reece was right about the outside world. How in the near future God would let it fall in a heap because of all the sin.

I hadn't seen much sin while I was walking from the station. Lots of dirty noisy factories, but not much sin. Maybe all the sin was going on inside.

At that moment I spotted some sin inside Denny's Salvage depot yard.

The tow-truck driver, the grown-up one, was coming out of an old wooden house that looked like it needed salvaging fairly urgently. He had a cigarette in one hand and a bottle of beer in the other. He must have forgotten it was only eight-fifteen in the morning.

He saw me, but didn't smile. Or wave.

Actually he scowled.

I thought about turning round and going home.

I couldn't.

I needed help from an expert, and he was the only salvage expert I knew.

'Yeah?' said the tow-truck driver, squinting through his own cigarette smoke as I walked towards him across the mud. 'What?'

Next to him was a pile of hulking car bodies. On the front of each rusting bonnet was the same badge. A lion.

Now I really knew how Daniel must have felt.

The tow-truck driver was looking at me more closely. Suddenly his eyes opened a bit wider and I saw that recognition was upon him.

'Jeez,' he said. 'You're a long way from heaven.'

He scowled again. 'Is God's loony chauffeur with you?'

I realised he meant Mr Gosper.

Quickly I shook my head.

'It's just me,' I said. 'Grace. Are you Mr Denny?'

He spat on the ground, which was probably why it was so muddy.

'That's me,' he said. 'But you've come to the wrong place.'

I didn't understand.

'I salvage wrecks,' he said. 'My wife salvages the tragic hairdos. Her salon's near the station.'

I knew I must have wisps out everywhere and probably a collapsed bun, but I resisted the temptation to repin it. I had something more important to do. Find the person here who might feel like helping me.

'I'm actually looking for your son,' I said. 'You know, the one with *Go Saints* written on his head.'

Mr Denny grunted.

'Pretty cool, eh?' he said. 'My wife did it. Follow me.'

We went inside the house, into a kind of kitchen, except there were no women there. Just Mr Denny's son sitting at a table scrubbing a greasy engine part with a very dirty toothbrush.

'Kyle,' said Mr Denny. 'Visitor. Name's Grace. Remember she's religious, so no swearing.'

He left us to it.

Kyle stared at me.

'Hi,' he said. 'If you've come for the chocolate, I haven't got it any more.'

I could hear Mr Denny outside, doing something with a power drill.

'I need your help,' I said.

Kyle looked anxious.

'It'll have to be quick,' he said. 'I've got to finish breakfast and leave for school in ten minutes.'

As fast as I could, I explained about Dad being booted out of church.

'He can be salvaged,' I said, 'I know he can.'

I pulled my bible project out of my bag and slid the folder across the table.

'There's lots of information in here to help you find him,' I said, opening the folder at The Book Of Dad.

Kyle stared at the folder.

He was tempted, I could tell. He glanced at me and I could tell he was feeling sympathetic.

But he shook his head.

'Sorry,' he said. 'My dad doesn't do that kind of salvaging. He's only interested in metal and bricks. And wood if it's not painted.'

Kyle gave me an apologetic look and poured himself a bowl of Coco Pops.

'Do you want some?' he said.

I shook my head. I didn't have time to explain that I'd have to boil them.

'You could try and persuade your dad,' I said.

'Tell him how this type of salvaging will help you learn new things and get on in life.'

Kyle thought about this.

He shook his head again.

Frantically I tried to think of what else I could say to change his mind.

'It doesn't matter if you and your dad don't believe in God,' I blurted out. 'I don't mind and God doesn't either.'

Kyle didn't say anything straight away. He frowned and finished chewing before he replied.

'I believe in God,' he said. 'So does my mum and dad. We just don't like Him much.'

I wasn't sure I'd heard right because Mr Denny was still drilling outside.

'Sometimes we hate Him,' said Kyle.

I had heard right. I could feel dust clogging my throat. I'd never been so aware that God could hear everything. I wished the drilling was louder.

'Why?' I said.

I knew God would probably prefer me to move on to another topic, but I had to know.

Kyle went over to an old dresser and pulled something out of a drawer. He put it on the table in front of me.

'Don't tell my dad I showed you this,' he said.

It was a battered photo album.

'That's why we don't like God,' said Kyle. 'Cos He lets that happen.'

I opened the album. It was full of photos of

wrecked cars. Not in the salvage yard outside. On streets and roads and highways. Some of them were so mangled you could hardly tell they were cars.

'What my dad reckons,' said Kyle, 'is if God's clever enough to make the whole world and everything, why would He let this happen to people if He wasn't a mongrel?'

I took a deep breath.

It was a reasonable question, except for the last bit. I tried to answer it.

'God lets us make our own mistakes,' I said.

Kyle seemed not to hear me. He was staring at the photo album.

I turned away. I couldn't look at the photos any more. I knew now why Kyle's dad was so keen for Kyle to get on in the world. So he wouldn't have to spend his life seeing this kind of thing.

'Their rellies come here sometimes,' said Kyle quietly. 'To look at the wrecks. Dad shows them and I make them tea.'

Kyle closed the album and put it back in the drawer. He looked out the window. 'Sometimes,' he said in an even quieter voice, 'when my dad goes speeding off on a call, I worry I'll be making tea for his rellies.'

I'd come here hoping Kyle could help me, but now, as I watched him gazing anxiously at the tow truck parked outside, I found myself wishing I could help him.

Which is probably why, out of the blue, I had an idea to help us both.

'If you salvage my dad,' I said, 'my mum will give you a reward.'

I was sure Mum wouldn't mind me saying that. Fairly sure.

'Not chocolate,' I said. 'Money. Enough for your dad to get his seatbelts fixed.'

Seatbelts couldn't be that expensive.

I could see Kyle was interested.

'And the brakes?' he said cautiously. 'And the muffler? They need fixing too.'

I wasn't sure what a muffler was, but I nodded again.

Kyle's face was glowing with nervous excitement. I could tell he was worried about pushing it too far, but at the same time he didn't want to stop. I'd seen that look on Dad's face in church heaps of times.

'And new tyres?' said Kyle. 'Me and my dad might have to drive all over the place to find your dad. It'd be dangerous doing that on bald tyres.'

I didn't want to stop now either.

'My family would pay really well,' I said.

I thought of a big amount and blurted it out. As soon as I heard myself say it, it didn't seem enough, so I said a bigger amount.

'OK,' said Kyle. 'Let's ask my dad.'

I was so relieved and excited I forgot myself and grabbed Kyle's arm.

'Do you think he'll say yes?' I asked. 'Even though this isn't metal and bricks?'

Kyle gave me a shy grin.

'I hope so,' he said. 'I'd like my dad to have the chance to learn new things and get on in life.'

Chapter 13

When I got home, all hell broke loose.

I knew I'd be in trouble when I went inside, but it actually started in the backyard.

Mark and Luke were playing Lions And Christians in the sandpit. Mark took one look at me and ran indoors.

'Mum,' he yelled. 'Grace is back.'

Luke sucked his plastic sword and stared at me.

'Dad kidnapped you,' he said. 'Dad's naughty.'

I started to explain that I hadn't even seen Dad, and that Dad would never do anything bad to us. But before I could finish, people ran out of the back door yelling at me.

'Grace,' shouted Uncle Vern. 'Come here.'

'Get inside,' roared Grandpop.

'Oh, Grace,' said Mum. 'How could you? It's been hours. We were frantic.'

They took me into the kitchen.

It was like the Spanish Inquisition. They sat me at the kitchen table and stood around me.

'How did you find him?' said Grandpop.

'Was it through his lawyer?' said Uncle Vern, holding up an official-looking letter.

'Did Dad come back here again last night?' said Mum.

I stared up at them, my head throbbing and my thoughts all over the place like fleeing Israelites.

I couldn't let them think Dad had kidnapped me. But I knew they wouldn't be any happier when I told them the truth. That I'd spent the day in the outside world rubbing shoulders with sinners and promising a bloke who drank beer for breakfast and a kid who didn't like God we'd give them a thousand dollars if they helped salvage Dad.

'We want you to be honest with us, Grace,' said Uncle Vern. 'We won't be cross.'

I wanted to be honest. I wanted to tell them that I was planning to be the most meek and obedient person in the whole church. Once Dad was back. But that first I had to do sins to find him.

I sighed.

If I said that, Grandpop would have a fit. Uncle Vern would have a migraine.

I decided to tell them the truth in a way that would save them as much pain as possible, and also save me from the sin of lying.

'I didn't see Dad,' I said quietly. 'I just went to find him.'

There was a silence. I hoped that would be enough truth for now.

'You poor child,' muttered Grandpop. 'He's lodged himself in your brain like a serpent.'

I opened my mouth to tell Grandpop he was wrong. That Dad had lodged himself in my heart like a great and loving dad. Plus, as far as I knew, serpents lived in deserts and jungles, not brains.

Before I could, Mum put her arms round me.

'Oh, love,' she said. 'We've been so worried. Cain and Turk are still out looking for you.'

'Sorry,' I said.

Uncle Vern got out his mobile.

'I'll call them,' he said, and went into the backyard.

Nannie handed me a cup of soup.

'There you go, dear,' she said. 'It's cabbage and yoghurt.'

While I sipped, I thought how lucky I was to have such a loving family. And how, deep down, they must be missing Dad too.

I flicked my eyes to the kitchen bench to see if Uncle Vern had left the letter from Dad's lawyer. If I could spot the lawyer's address, that would be useful information to give to Kyle and his dad. But the letter wasn't there. Uncle Vern must have taken it with him.

I wished I could tell Mum about Kyle and Mr Denny. Poor Mum. Her face was tired with worry. If she knew Dad was going to be salvaged, lo, bulk grief would be lifted from her heart.

While I was trying to work out if I should risk it, Grandpop put his hands on my shoulders and closed his eyes.

'We beseech you, O Lord,' he said. 'Free this innocent child from the misguided evil influence of the man who was once her father. Amen.'

'Amen,' whispered Nannie.

It wasn't fair. I knew Grandpop was only saying that because he loved me, but I was starting to get a bit fed up with people putting me in their prayers when I didn't want to be.

I decided not to tell Mum that Dad was going to be salvaged by outsiders. Grandpop might find out. And then the church elders might get even angrier with Dad.

'Alright, love,' Mum said to me. 'When you've finished your soup, get upstairs and pack up your room.'

I looked at her, confused.

She was giving me a pleading look.

Why? My room wasn't that untidy.

Then I saw what Nannie was doing. Packing plates and cups into cardboard boxes.

'We're moving house,' said Mum, trying to sound like it was a good thing.

My brain went Israelite again.

'Moving house?' I said.

'You heard your mother,' said Grandpop in his church-elder voice.

Anxiety was upon me big time.

'Where are we going?' I said to Mum.

'The address doesn't matter,' said Grandpop.

Mum was giving me the pleading look again. I beheld she was torn asunder, kind of. She didn't want to move house, but at the same time she didn't want to upset the elders in case it made things worse for Dad.

'But,' I said, my voice squeaky with panic, 'how will Dad be able to . . .?'

I stopped myself.

It was too late. Grandpop was looking at me very sternly.

'How will he be able to find you?' said Grandpop. 'That's the whole point. He won't.'

Chapter 14

On my first day in the new house I needed some advice, so I had a word with God.

I told Him I was very grateful to have my own bedroom, even though I was finding being locked in it doing Bible solitary since breakfast a bit frustrating.

'Please don't take that personally,' I said.

I asked God to forgive Grandpop and the other church elders for punishing Dad by hiding us in a secret house.

'I don't think they realise how mean they're being,' I said. 'And pig-headed.'

Finally I asked God a question.

'When you're locked in an upstairs room,' I said, 'and you can't see any street signs out the window, and you couldn't see any last night when you arrived because it was dark, and you couldn't memorise the route from your old house because you didn't recognise any landmarks after the Breezy Whale carwash, how can you find out the address of the new house so Dad knows where to come when he's ready to be meek and obedient?'

It was a difficult question, but I knew God was used to those.

I thanked God for listening. Almost immediately He gave me an idea and I got busy. For I remembered what Dad had taught me. Don't sit back and wait for God to do it all. Ask for His advice, but be prepared to do the hard yards yourself.

Which I was.

I turned to page one of the Bible. Dad reckoned the Bible was more a book of advice than a book of rules, and I was pretty sure that somewhere in it I'd find the clue I needed.

When I was halfway down page two, I heard a faint tinkling sound. I looked around the room. Outside the window, crouching on the ledge and staring at me through the glass, was a kitten.

My first thought was that the poor thing was in danger. It was high up. If it slipped and fell . . .

I was sure God cared about animals as much as humans, but there wasn't a lot He could do once they were airborne.

I went to the window and carefully slid it open, trying not to scare the kitten. It was a beautiful colour, sort of yellowy gold, like a little lion.

'Hello,' I said. 'You're a good climber.'

There was a tree overhanging the house, but the kitten didn't seem in a hurry to go back down.

'Come in,' I said.

Before I could pick it up, it jumped over my hands and onto my bed.

'Make yourself at home,' I said.

The tinkling was coming from a bell around its neck. As I reached out to stroke the kitten, I noticed something else hanging from its collar. A small metal disc with engraved words.

I looked more closely.

It was an address.

28 Spinoza Crescent, Clayton Lakes.

The kitten was staring up at me like it was waiting for something to happen. My brain to start working, for example.

Of course.

Spinoza Crescent must be the street we were in. If the kitten lived next door in number 28, I was in either number 26 or number 30. Even if the kitten was from across the street, this house was probably somewhere between numbers 20 and 40. Which was enough information for a clever and determined dad like Dad.

'Thank you,' I said to the kitten.

It gave a few small miaows and peed on my bed.

Fair enough, I thought. Even messengers from God have bladders.

I poured some soup from my cup into the saucer and gave it to the kitten.

'It's lentil and ricotta,' I said. 'Nannie could work

for Campbell's soup if our church allowed women to have jobs.'

Then I got to work.

I tore a couple of pages out of an exercise book. On one page I wrote a letter to Kyle and Mr Denny asking them to tell Dad about Spinoza Crescent as soon as they found him. With sticky tape I made an envelope from the other piece of paper and addressed it to Denny's Salvage. In the corner, where the stamp would normally go, I wrote 'please post' and drew a begging face.

'You may not have been warned about this bit,' I said to the kitten.

I emptied my pencil case and put the letter into it. Then, carefully and gently, I tied the pencil case to the kitten's back by looping a shoelace several times under the kitten's tummy. I knotted the shoelace and made sure it was tight enough to hold the pencil case on, but not so tight the kitten couldn't breathe or digest lentil soup.

'Sorry,' I said. 'It's probably a bit uncomfortable, but please don't try to take it off.'

I let go of the kitten.

It rolled around on the carpet, claws scrabbling, trying to get the pencil case off its back.

I let it try. God encourages humans to think for themselves, so it's only fair that animals should have the same opportunity.

'You can take it off later,' I said, 'but I'd be really grateful if you leave it on till you get home.'

I made sure that the knot in the shoelace was still tied.

The kitten wriggled away from me, bolted to the other side of the room, glared at me, then leaped out the window.

'Careful,' I called. 'Don't forget this is upstairs.'

I hurried over to the window and looked down, worry upon me.

What if the kitten wasn't a messenger from God? What if it was just an ordinary kitten thrown off balance by a pencil case and now it was lying down there, dead? Killing an innocent animal with stationery was a sin that would haunt me forever.

But it wasn't to be, for suddenly I saw the kitten, scampering down the tree, pencil case still on its back.

'Thanks,' I called, my voice wobbly with relief.

The kitten disappeared into next-door's garden. I closed the window and went back to Bible solitary.

All I could do now was wait.

Suddenly I missed Dad so much it was like a stab in the guts. I tried to imagine what it would be like to never see him again.

I couldn't.

It was as impossible as trying to imagine what it would be like not to believe in God.

I couldn't do that either.

I always had and I knew I always would.

To make myself feel better, I pretended I was

on the back lawn with Dad, asking interesting questions.

If I was a girl who didn't believe in God, I asked Dad, would I have tied a letter to a kitten in the hope that a complete stranger would find it and be generous enough to stick a stamp on it and get it into a post box by 6pm?

Dad thought about this.

Probably not, he said.

I agreed.

Chapter 15

And so it came to pass that I couldn't sleep properly for the next two nights, that's how anxious I was about Dad.

Both nights I didn't conk out until about 3am, so I slept in late.

Or tried to.

The second morning my eyes opened very early because Mum was shaking me.

'Mum,' I groaned. 'I haven't had enough sleep.'

'When you hear what I've got to tell you,' she said, 'you won't want to sleep.'

Suddenly I was awake.

'Is Dad back?' I said, sitting up.

Mum shook her head.

Poor Mum. I could tell from the troubled skin under her eyes that she hadn't slept much either.

'Not yet,' she said. 'But soon.'

I gave her a hug. It was good of her to try and cheer us up.

'Very soon,' I said. 'Because God is giving us the strength to get Dad back.'

Mum just kept hugging me.

After a while I felt my shoulder getting damp.

'It's OK,' I whispered. 'He is.'

I decided to risk telling Mum about Kyle and Mr Denny and how Dad would soon be salvaged. But before I could, Mum lifted her head and behold, she was smiling under her tears.

'Grandpop has sent Dad a letter,' she said.

I stared at her. A ray of weak early-morning sunlight was coming in through the curtains and Mum's hair was shining faintly golden like the kitten's fur.

'A letter?' I said, excitement rising inside me.

'Dad's lawyer was threatening to go to the Family Court and start a big fight,' said Mum. 'Which would be terrible for you kids. So Grandpop decided to try and end the conflict by writing to Dad.'

Relief surged inside me like the Red Sea, because I didn't have to be an Old Testament prophet to guess what the letter said.

'Grandpop's telling Dad he can come back?' I squealed. 'Grandpop's telling Dad if he stops getting into arguments and promises to be meek and obedient, he won't be expelled any more?'

Mum nodded, her wet face beaming.

Yes.

I felt like jumping out of bed and doing cartwheels. Delight was abundant within me. But

I stayed where I was, partly because I couldn't do cartwheels and partly because I wanted to keep hugging Mum.

I was tearful with happiness myself.

Dad would be back soon.

'Grandpop's going to read the letter to everyone in church tomorrow,' said Mum. 'You'll get to hear it then.'

Bountiful. They were allowing me out of my room to go to church. Things were almost back to normal.

'Are we going back to our old house?' I asked.

'If Grandpop's letter works,' Mum said.

She smiled again. But just for a moment she looked a tiny bit uncertain. I wished I could give her bulk faith that Grandpop would write a good letter and Dad would do what it commanded for all our sakes.

'It will work,' I said.

'Of course it will,' she said.

Mum and I lay quietly together. After a while Mum dropped off to sleep. I was glad because she needed it.

I snuggled into her and had a quick word to God about the church elders and how I'd been unkind to them lately in my thoughts.

'Forgive me,' I said. 'For now I know they're not pig-headed meanies after all.'

I must have gone back to sleep too, because the next

thing I knew Mum wasn't there and somebody or something was tapping on my window.

For a dopey moment I thought the kitten was back to collect the money for the stamp.

Then I woke up properly and saw the shape of someone's head through the curtain. Which was weird. A person, this high off the ground?

I squeezed my eyes shut and opened them again. It was definitely a person. And they were still tapping on the glass.

I hurried over to the window and pulled back the curtain.

And blinked in surprise.

It was Kyle.

He was standing on a ladder, looking at me anxiously. The breeze was ruffling his spiky hair, all except for the shaved bit.

He held up an envelope.

Amazement was upon me as I realised it was my letter. Somebody must have found it tied to the kitten and posted it. Which was a miracle.

'Thank you,' I whispered to God.

Kyle was saying something through the glass, but Mark and Luke were making such a racket smiting each other downstairs that I couldn't hear.

I slid the window open.

'Are you OK?' said Kyle.

'Yes,' I said, still a bit dazed to see him. 'Thanks.'

'We've come to rescue you,' he said.

I stared at him. And at Mr Denny down below, holding the bottom rungs. I hadn't expected this.

'You said you were being kept prisoner,' Kyle went on. 'In your letter.'

It was true, I had mentioned being locked in, but I was pretty sure I hadn't actually used the word 'prisoner'.

'So we've come to rescue you,' said Kyle. 'My dad reckons kids shouldn't be locked up. That's child abuse. And what they did to your dad wasn't fair either, so my dad says we'll find him for half price.'

I didn't know what to say. It was so kind. They weren't even in our church.

I wanted to invite them in and thank them and give them some soup. But I realised I couldn't. If Grandpop found I'd brought outsiders into the house, he'd probably blame Dad.

And change his mind.

And rip up his letter of forgiveness.

Even me being seen with Kyle was risking Grandpop's wrath.

'Thanks so much,' I said. 'But I made a mistake. I don't actually need to be rescued. Thanks anyway.'

I peered anxiously down into the street again. The red tow truck was parked outside the house. Grandpop couldn't miss it.

'It's an incredibly kind thought,' I said to Kyle. 'But could you go now?'

Kyle was staring at me, puzzled.

'Things have got better,' I explained. 'We can salvage Dad ourselves now. Sorry.'

Kyle was starting to look hurt.

I felt awful.

And that was before Grandpop's voice roared up from below.

'Hey, you up there. What do you think you're doing? Get down off that ladder.'

I ducked back from the window.

'Keep your shirt on,' I heard Mr Denny say to Grandpop. 'We're here to salvage your roof. You've ordered a new metal roof, right?'

While Grandpop yelled that he hadn't ordered a new roof of any kind, and threatened to call the police if Mr Denny didn't get his ladder off our house immediately, Kyle looked at me.

He was very hurt now.

'I thought you needed our help,' he said. 'I told my dad I really wanted to help you. We gave up footy for this.'

'Please go,' I begged.

I closed my eyes so I wouldn't have to look at Kyle's face, and waited while he slowly clanged his way down the ladder.

As soon as I heard the ladder being dragged away from the window, I closed the curtains and dived into bed.

I lay there, guilt and regret upon me, listening to Mr Denny and Grandpop yelling at each other.

Kyle didn't dob me in once.

That made me cry.

After the tow truck roared away, and I'd dried my eyes, Grandpop came into my room. He sat on the bed and stroked my head.

'Those fools didn't even have the right street,' he said. 'Godless and idiotic, what a tragic combination. The outside world is full of lost confused souls, Grace. Helpless fools with minds so open, they're just inviting evil in. That's what we're protecting you from.'

'Thank you, Grandpop,' I said.

But inside I felt awful.

Grandpop was wrong.

Kyle and his dad weren't helpless fools, and they did have the right street, and the only hurtful thing they'd invited into their hearts was me.

Chapter 16

'Are we there yet?' said Mark.

'Are we?' said Luke.

Uncle Vern didn't answer. He must have been too busy driving. Mum didn't say anything either. Probably too excited to speak.

'We'll be there soon,' I said to the twins.

I was very excited too. Today was the day Dad was going to agree to be meek and obedient and be officially accepted back into our church. Well, I was pretty sure it would be today. Why else would Grandpop read his letter to Dad out at the service?

'Singing,' shrieked Mark.

'I heard it first,' yelled Luke.

'Shhh, you two,' said Mum.

Mark and Luke were right. I could hear it myself now, distant voices on the breeze coming in through the car window.

The singing in our church always travelled a long way. Grandpop reckoned it was because we were the chosen ones. Dad reckoned it was the 20,000 watt sound system in the building. Our church used to be a warehouse, like the home-lighting warehouse next door to it and the carpet warehouse on the other side. Then one day the elders reckoned God told them to knock down the warehouse church and build one with stadium seating and a sound system He could hear.

We drove in through the church gates.

'G'day, George,' Uncle Vern called out.

The church security guard gave us a wave.

The car jolted as we drove over the security hump. The one with the row of sharp daggers that could pop up and slash the tyres of outsiders who tried to drive into our church carpark without an invitation.

We parked. The singing was very loud now.

'We're a bit late,' I said, puzzled that Mum and Uncle Vern didn't seem worried the service had started. Mum normally hated that.

'We're fine,' said Uncle Vern. 'We're having a little ceremony today and the elders asked us to arrive at this time.'

Mum looked at him.

'You didn't tell me that,' she said.

'It'll be fine,' said Uncle Vern.

I knew it would. For I knew what sort of ceremony he was talking about. One where a dad and his family were reunited forever.

Mum squeezed my arm. But she wasn't looking

as excited as she should have been, and that made me a bit puzzled.

We got out of the car and went into the building.

The singing stopped. It felt strange, walking into a completely silent church. Everyone was looking at me. But then something really nice happened. As I walked past the rows of seats, people started patting me and stroking me and saying kind things.

'We love you, Grace.'

'God bless you, dear Grace.'

'You're very precious to us, child.'

Some of the people I didn't know, but some of them I did.

'I'm serious, Grace. You are so my most holy and biblical friend.'

It was lovely, and by the time Uncle Vern told me to stop walking, I wasn't feeling nervous at all, just excited at the thought of seeing Dad.

'Stand here,' said Uncle Vern, 'and we'll get started.'

I waited in the aisle. Mum and the twins sat down and I stood on tip-toe, trying to see where Dad was in the church.

Grandpop was down the front on the stage, at the microphone. He cleared his throat. He always did that when he was speaking at a service.

'O Lord,' he said, 'one of your precious chosen few has strayed, but today has returned to you in meekness and obedience. Amen.'

While everyone else said Amen, I peered around, trying to catch a glimpse of Dad.

I still couldn't see him.

Then I realised that on the stage, Grandpop was holding his arms out towards me.

'Welcome, Grace,' he said in his church voice. 'In meekness and obedience you have returned to us.'

I stared at him.

Me?

What about Dad?

'To demonstrate your repentence,' Grandpop said, 'you may now come forward and humble yourself before those you have offended.'

I didn't know what he was talking about.

Where was Dad?

Grandpop was beckoning me towards the stage.

Dazed, I went down the aisle.

And lo, I found myself standing at the very front of the church. Where I'd never been before. Where only the elders and other mega-important holy people went.

The front row of seats, where the elders were sitting, was very close.

I couldn't help staring.

The elders had their shoes and socks off. The pants legs of their suits were rolled up to just below their knees.

Next to each knobbly pair of feet was a plastic bowl of water.

'You may now humble yourself before those

you have offended,' repeated Grandpop in a tone of voice that sounded like there was something I should be doing.

Confusion was upon me.

Grandpop stepped forward and quickly, one by one, pulled out all my hairpins. My bun unravelled and my hair tumbled down to my waist.

As he pulled out the last hairpin, Grandpop put his mouth close to my ear.

'Wash their feet,' he said.

I stared at him.

I stared at the feet.

And lo, slowly it dawned on me. In the Bible, when a person, who's usually a female person, has offended another person, who's usually a male person, she washes his feet to say sorry.

I glanced across the rows of seats to where Mum was sitting. I could see from her face she hadn't been expecting this and I could see she was anxious about it.

So was I.

I knelt next to the first pair of feet, which belonged to Mr Craddock, who was Grandpop's lawyer. His feet were bony with shiny yellow lumpy bits on them that weren't toenails. I knew the lumpy bits were probably from poor Mr Craddock being on his feet a lot in court, but my guts still went wobbly at the thought of touching them.

I made myself.

I decided it must be a test. The elders must be

checking to see if Dad had permanently warped me with his dangerous ideas and his dark and sinful questions. I had to show everyone I could be meek and obedient too.

Next to Mr Craddock's plastic bowl of water was a bar of soap. I made some lather and rubbed it onto his toes. It was like touching a bony frog. I hoped I wasn't tickling him.

I glanced up at Mr Craddock's face. I needn't have worried. He was staring into the distance with a serious expression and wasn't giggling at all.

I lifted his feet over the bowl and sloshed the soap off, careful not to splash water onto the church carpet.

I looked around for a towel.

There wasn't one.

That was when I remembered something else about feet-washing in the Bible. When a biblical female washes a biblical man's feet, she usually dries them with her hair.

I took a deep breath and a big handful of my own hair and kneeled closer to Mr Craddock's dripping feet and started drying them.

There's a reason, I quickly discovered, why God gave us cotton. By the time Mr Craddock's feet were half-dry, my hair was damp and my neck was aching worse than after an all-night prayer meeting.

Wearily I glanced at the other feet waiting for me. Six pairs.

I moved on to the next pair, wishing Dad would

appear with an encouraging hug and a hairdryer. The next feet were Mr Taylor's. He owned a tyre warehouse, and from the smell and the black stuff under his toenails, he must have changed most of the tyres with his bare toes.

Behind me, Grandpop was talking to the church members. While I washed and rinsed, I started listening to what he was saying to take my mind off the feet.

'A tragic loss to our church,' he was saying into the microphone. 'Even more tragic is when a rebellious adult tries to steal his children from us. But fear not, friends, a solution has been found. Yesterday the troubled soul in question was sent a letter that I feel confident will resolve this problem and allow those children to sleep peacefully. Let me read the letter to you.'

Grandpop cleared his throat again. I tried to rinse Mr Taylor's feet quietly so I wouldn't miss any of the letter welcoming Dad back.

'*Dear Mr Hillgrove,*' read Grandpop. '*Stop trying to contact me and Mum and the twins. You chose Satan over us and the church. So now you don't have a church or a family. Leave us alone. We don't ever want to see you again. Your former daughter, Grace.*'

Only God kept me breathing because every single part of my body was in shock.

I hardly noticed as Mr Taylor's foot slipped out of my hands and fell into the bowl with a splash.

How could he?

How could my own grandfather commit such an evil act of forgery?

Suddenly fury blazed through me and I was on my feet.

'No,' I screamed.

'It's not true,' shouted another voice.

Mum's.

A buzz went through the church. I lunged towards Grandpop to snatch the letter and tear it up. Then I remembered it was only a copy. Dad had already got it. I couldn't bear to think about that, about what Dad must have felt when he read it.

Uncle Vern was striding towards me.

I turned and ran.

I barged through a fire exit into the kitchen area.

Uncle Vern was calling my name, but I only stopped for a second. Just long enough to grab a big pair of scissors from the draining board. Then I sprinted to the far end of the kitchen and into the toilet.

I locked myself in.

I'd read somewhere that hair is easier to cut when it's wet. It was true. By the time Uncle Vern started rattling the door handle and telling me to come out, half my hair was on the floor.

The scissors were very big and I had to use both hands, but every snip sent another tangled rope of damp hair plummeting.

When I'd finished, I dropped the scissors and scooped up my hair. I unlocked the door and sprinted past startled Uncle Vern into the church.

They were having the service as if nothing had happened. All except Mum and the twins, who were up the back being hustled out by Cain and Turk and some others.

The elders still had their shoes and socks off. I dumped my hair on the floor in front of them.

'Wash your own feet,' I yelled.

The elders looked stunned.

So did the other church members. Some of them grabbed each other. Poor things. My angry yelling was bad enough, but when they saw my haircut they gasped. In our church it was a sin for women and girls to cut their hair, except to trim split ends.

All I had left were split ends, all over my head in short spiky clumps.

I didn't care.

There was something else I wanted to say to the elders of our church.

'You mongrels had better expel me too,' I yelled, 'because I'm not going to heaven without my dad.'

Chapter 17

In our church they didn't expel kids who did big sins. Instead they made you live in the family room behind a sheet.

In exile.

Grandpop strung a washing line across the room and hung a sheet over it to make a cloth wall. He and Uncle Vern carried my bed down and put it behind the sheet.

I was in a polyester and cotton jail cell.

My meals were slid under the sheet on a tray. The door to the downstairs bathroom was inside my cell, so I didn't even get human contact on the way to the toilet. I wasn't allowed any contact with anyone. They wouldn't tell me how long I was in for, and I hoped it wasn't until my hair grew back.

'Why don't you lock me in my bedroom again?' I said to Grandpop as he checked the knots at each end of the washing line.

He didn't reply.

He wouldn't even tell me where Mum was.

He only said one thing to me, very sternly.

'While you're here,' he said, 'have a think about why these terrible things have befallen us. See if you think God might be punishing this family because some of this family have lost faith in Him.'

I glared at Grandpop.

'Dad hasn't lost faith in God,' I said. 'No way.'

Grandpop gave me a long look.

'I don't just mean your father,' he said.

A little while later, Mum crept in to see me.

'Oh, love,' she said sadly as we hugged. 'Look at you.'

She stroked the tufts on my head.

'Sorry,' I said.

'Don't be,' said Mum. 'What they did to you in church was a disgrace. And if I'd had any idea that Grandpop was going to write a letter like that, I'd have tried to stop him.'

She sighed. I could see she wasn't completely sure if she'd have succeeded.

'Will I have to stay behind this sheet for long?' I asked.

'Not if I have any say in it,' replied Mum.

She sighed again.

Her hair wasn't in great shape either. Wisps out all over the place. I could tell from her face she was worrying about the same thing as me. The bulk woe that must have come upon Dad after he read the letter.

'We have to contact Dad,' I said. 'We have to let him know the letter wasn't from me, and that we still love him and want him.'

Mum nodded.

'I'll do my best,' she said. 'I'll try to find out the address of his lawyer.'

Suddenly she was looking more determined than I'd ever seen her. And I wanted to give her all the help I could.

Keeping my voice low, I told her about Kyle and his dad. I explained that if she looked in my school bag, she'd find the piece of paper with their address and phone number.

Mum was staring at me.

Shock was upon her.

'I wasn't very nice to poor Kyle and Mr Denny yesterday,' I said. 'But they might still help us when they hear how serious things have got.'

Mum recovered from her shock.

She nodded and squeezed my arm, and I could tell from the look on her face that to get Dad back, she'd ring up every outsider in the world if she had to.

By that evening I'd worked out why the elders hadn't locked me in my bedroom.

In your bedroom you're alone and lonely.

In the family room it's worse.

The rest of the family are just a few metres away.

You can hear them and even see them if you peek round the sheet. But they have to pretend you're not there.

'Grace is hiding behind the washing,' said Mark at the dinner table.

I knew they were having dinner because I could hear their knives and forks.

'Eat your fish fingers, boys,' said Mum wearily.

I tried to hear in her voice whether she was weary from having long phone conversations with Mr Denny, or just weary from worry.

'Why is Grace?' said Luke.

Mum didn't answer.

'Grace is being punished,' said Grandpop. 'You have to pretend she's not here.'

'Is God punishing her?' said Mark.

'Yes,' said Grandpop.

'Why is He?' said Luke. 'Did she leave her room in a mess?'

I smiled sadly and said a silent thank you that at least I could hear Mark and Luke, even though today we couldn't save our peas and gravy till last and do Israelite races across the Red Sea together like we normally did.

Dad must have been missing them so much.

After dinner the sheet rippled and behold, Delilah and Liam ducked into my cell.

'You poor thing,' said Delilah, looking around.

'You are so judged. They totally haven't even given you a hair dryer.'

'What are you doing here?' I said, sitting up on my bed. 'You'll get into big trouble if you're caught.'

'We're legal,' said Liam.

I looked at them, puzzled.

'We're like on a mission,' said Delilah. 'Your Grandpop asked us to save your immortal soul. Which I am so honoured to do.'

'He didn't say that,' muttered Liam. 'He just asked us to set you a good example of being holy.'

'Same,' said Delilah. 'Let's sing some hymns.'

She started singing one.

It was kind of her. I waited till she'd finished.

'Delilah,' I said. 'It's nice to see you, but I don't need saving, thanks anyway.'

'See?' said Liam to Delilah. 'Too late. Satan city. I told you.'

Delilah started singing another hymn.

'Please,' I said. 'Don't.'

Delilah stopped singing. She put her hands on my head.

'We beseech you, O Lord,' she cried out. 'Save this poor ungodly kid, cos she didn't mean it, I'm serious.'

I rolled my eyes.

Delilah's shoulders slumped.

'This is so not working,' she said.

'Told you,' said Liam.

Delilah looked at me mournfully.

'We tried,' she said. 'But the evil in you is too bulk. The Lord has lost it with you totally. You poor thing. Can I have your hair conditioner?'

Later that night I heard Mum arguing with Grandpop. They must have thought I was asleep.

'He's my husband,' said Mum. 'I've got a right to speak to him.'

'I'm an elder in this church,' said Grandpop, 'and I forbid you to put your soul at risk by consorting with outsiders.'

'I'm not consorting,' said Mum. 'I just want to tell Gavin we still love him.'

'Don't you dare disobey me,' said Grandpop.

They must have lowered their voices because after that I couldn't hear what they were saying. But I could hear Grandpop getting angrier, and Mum too.

Suddenly there was the sound of a slap.

I sat up in bed, shocked. In our family we never hit each other. Except when Mark and Luke did it, but that was only smiting.

For a crazy moment I wondered if Mum had slapped Grandpop. Dad reckoned Grandpop had been bossing Mum around since she was a little girl, and if you push people too far they can lose it. Look at Joan of Arc.

I slid out of bed and peeked round the sheet.

Mum and Grandpop were standing at the other

end of the family room. I was wrong. Mum was holding her face. Grandpop was glaring at her, his arms folded in a very strict way.

Poor Mum. Her shoulders were hunched and she was staring at the floor. She looked more like a little kid than a mum.

I wanted to go and comfort her so much. But I stayed where I was. I still had a desperate hope that Dad would turn up and beg for forgiveness, and I wanted to be meek and obedient for his sake.

'If you ever disobey me again,' said Grandpop to Mum, 'if I ever catch you trying to involve outsiders in church affairs again, you will be expelled. Just like that evil husband of yours. And you know what that will mean.'

Mum didn't say anything.

'It will mean,' continued Grandpop, 'that the church will use its lawyers to make sure you never see your children again.'

Mum put her face in her hands.

I lay back down on my bed, shock and misery upon me.

Grandpop was right. Terrible things were happening to our family. But it wasn't God who was making them happen.

It was Grandpop.

Suddenly I knew what I had to do.

It was the only thing left.

I talked to God.

'Please,' I said, 'I need Your help. We all do.

I know I'm not meant to ask You to fix things, and I wouldn't normally, but I'm desperate. Please bring my dad home. Please put love back into Grandpop's heart. Please make us a family again.'

At the other end of the dark house I could hear the faint sound of Mum crying.

'Please,' I said to God.

Chapter 18

Tribulation is like trouble, only worse.

Your insides feel afflicted, and your mind feels anxious, and when you're waiting for God to make it go away and He hasn't yet, it feels really bad.

I had a lot of tribulation upon me the next day.

For the whole morning and afternoon the only person who visited my cell was Nannie, and that was just to slide my meals under the sheet.

'I know you can't speak to me, Nannie,' I said. 'But thank you.'

Poor Nannie gave a sob and I heard her footsteps hurry out of the family room.

I could hear everyone else too, further away. Mark and Luke outside, smiting. Mum and Grandpop upstairs, arguing.

On the tray, as well as my breakfast, was a box. I picked it up. It was one of Nannie's jigsaw puzzles. Her Paris one. All Nannie's jigsaws were of sinful places. Dad reckoned it was because she enjoyed pulling them apart afterwards.

After breakfast I did the jigsaw.

As I clicked Paris together piece by piece, I beheld that it looked like an interesting place, not a sinful one. I didn't pull it apart. I decided I'd like to visit it one day. With Mum and Mark and Luke.

And Dad.

I spent the rest of the day in bed, waiting for God to fix things and make us a family again.

I pretended I was Jonah. The Bible reckons Jonah was inside a whale for three days and three nights, and not once did he lose his faith.

It was hard for both of us. Jonah had to have faith he wouldn't get dissolved by stomach juices or smothered by half-chewed squid. My job was a bit different. I had to have faith that God would bring Dad back to us.

And I did.

I kept it going the whole day.

Right up until the evening, when Grandpop and Uncle Vern and Mr Gosper came to see me.

I was surprised to see Mr Gosper. He hardly ever visited our house.

Mr Gosper and Grandpop and Uncle Vern squeezed into my polyester and cotton cubicle and surrounded me and made me stay in bed and stood there giving me lectures on meekness and obedience.

Grandpop and Uncle Vern kicked it off, and that

was bad enough, but when Mr Gosper started to boss me around too, unease and indignation were upon me.

'This rebellious behaviour has got to stop, young lady,' said Mr Gosper. He smoothed his long wisps of grey hair over his head. 'You're bringing shame on this family and discrediting us in the eyes of the Lord.'

I was confused.

Was he talking about my family or the church family?

'I won't stand for it,' said Mr Gosper.

It couldn't be my family because he wasn't even in my family.

'Your mother has tried her best,' said Mr Gosper. 'But no woman can be a good mother without the right man beside her. Little wonder you've turned out the way you have.'

Uncle Vern was nodding with a sad frown.

'I'm afraid that's right,' he said.

Grandpop was nodding too, sternness upon him.

'What this young lady needs, Neville,' he said to Mr Gosper, 'is to learn respect for the Lord.'

'What you need, young lady,' said Mr Gosper to me, 'is to learn respect for the Lord.'

I couldn't stand it any longer. First Mr Gosper had insulted Mum and Dad, now he was bad-mouthing my friendship with God.

'You can't tell me what to do,' I muttered to Mr Gosper. 'You're not my father.'

There was a long silence.

'Not yet,' said Grandpop.

There was another long silence while I tried to work out what Grandpop meant.

I couldn't.

'What do you mean, not yet?' I said.

Mr Gosper opened his mouth to say something, but Grandpop put a hand on his arm and Mr Gosper closed his mouth.

'Your parents' marriage is over,' Grandpop said to me. 'Your mother and the man who used to be your father are getting a divorce, and Mr Gosper has kindly offered to marry your mother.'

I sat up and just stared at them.

Then I flung myself at Mr Gosper and tried to claw his hair out.

They held me down on the bed. I struggled and kicked for a long time. Grandpop prayed for me in his church voice.

Finally, when I was exhausted, I stopped.

They let go of me.

I put my head under the pillow and waited for them to leave.

In the middle of the night Mum crept into my cell and squeezed into bed next to me.

'I'm sorry,' she whispered. 'I'm so sorry.'

'Don't do it, Mum,' I begged. 'Don't divorce Dad. God will keep us together. You won't lose us kids.'

'Oh, love,' said Mum.

She started crying. I did too.

'Grace,' said Mum. 'I don't want to divorce Dad. He wants to divorce me.'

I stared at her in the darkness, disbelief upon me. And panic.

'It was the letter, wasn't it?' I said. 'Dad wants a divorce because he thinks we hate him.'

Mum held my face in her hands.

'No, Grace,' she said. 'I don't think it's that. I think he's doing it out of love for us. I think he accepts we can't leave the church, and he knows the elders would hate me staying married to him, so he's trying to make things as easy for us here as he can.'

Mum started crying again.

I lay there, holding her, trying to imagine what Dad must be feeling after deciding something like that.

Miserable.

Lonely.

Full of tribulation.

It wasn't hard to imagine because I was feeling those things too.

'He didn't even tell me himself,' sobbed Mum. 'Because he knew I wouldn't agree. His lawyer rang and spoke to Grandpop.'

I wished desperately that Dad was here with us. So we could talk about all this. So we could go back to how we used to be.

But he wasn't.

And God wasn't with us either. Since I'd asked for His help, things had got worse.

God was ignoring us.

Suddenly I knew why. There was only one possible explanation.

Grandpop was right. All this terrible misery in our family was happening because God thought me and Dad had lost faith in Him.

God was punishing us.

Which meant there was only one thing I could do to change things. Find a way to prove to God that my love for Him and faith in Him and devotion to Him were as strong as ever.

I had to be like Jonah, but in real life.

Chapter 19

I needed a whale.

There weren't any near our place, so I settled for the next best thing, the Breezy Whale carwash.

Luckily it opened early.

I'd left the house at 4am because Dad had told me once that's when humans have their deepest sleep and I didn't want anyone to hear me breaking the downstairs bathroom window to get out.

I stood outside the Breezy Whale, watching a car disappear slowly into the mist of froth and spray, while I planned my next move.

Jonah had spent three days and three nights inside the whale's tummy. What I needed was an ordeal as dangerous as that, so God could see I had total faith in Him. And also, when God kept me safe, so the church elders could see that even sinners like me and Dad were precious in God's eyes.

There was one problem.

I couldn't do the whole three days and three

nights because the Breezy Whale was only open from 7am to 10pm.

I spoke to God about it. I explained that my ordeal was going to be shorter than Jonah's, but that didn't mean my faith was any less than his.

'Probably the reason Jonah's ordeal took three days and three nights,' I said to God, 'was because he was way out in the middle of the ocean instead of just on Steve Waugh Boulevard.'

I walked up the concrete slope to the gaping mouth of the carwash. The car I'd been watching had finished its ordeal, and the massive plastic strips were hanging there, dripping and gently swaying, waiting for their next grubby visitor.

Now I was up close, I was pleased to see that the inside of the carwash did look a bit like a whale's tummy, if you ignored the fluorescent lights and the sign advertising liquid wax.

The giant plastic strips looked scary, which was good. I knew from the Bible that fear was an important part of an ordeal.

I reached into my pocket and took out the dollar coins I'd brought. I put five of them into the slot and walked towards the green light, committing myself to the care of the Lord.

'Stop,' boomed a mighty voice high above me.

I stopped.

I looked up.

I waited for further instructions.

But the voice was silent. All I could hear was

a faint whistling sound coming from a big metal loudspeaker bolted to the roof.

'What d'ya think ya doin'?'

The voice wasn't coming from on high, it was coming from behind me.

I turned. A chubby bloke in an orange jacket was sprinting over.

'You wander in there, girlie,' panted the bloke, 'and the auto-safety shut-off image-sensor in that camera'll have us closed down for the rest of the morning.'

I looked up to where he was pointing. Bolted to the roof near the loudspeaker was a video camera.

I sighed.

'What ya doin' anyhow?' said the bloke.

I decided not to explain. He looked like a nice person, but he probably wouldn't like the idea of his carwash being used for religious purposes.

He pointed at my school bag.

'Project?' he said.

I tried to give him a smile, like you do when you don't want to commit the sin of lying. But I was finding it hard to smile. Everything was going wrong. God had lost His temper with me and now He didn't even want to give me the chance to prove myself.

That's what I thought until I saw the name tag the bloke was wearing on his carwash jacket.

Then I did smile, because I realised God was just telling me I'd chosen the wrong ordeal. And now I knew exactly which ordeal He wanted me to undergo.

It was written on the name tag.

Daniel.

I was feeling pretty nervous by the time I got to Denny's Salvage.

I knew Kyle and his dad would probably be angry when they saw me. I couldn't blame them. They'd opened their hearts to me and lo, I'd been totally ungodly back. They had every right to chuck rusty bits of metal at me if they wanted to. I just hoped they'd control themselves long enough to give me the technical information I needed.

The salvage yard gates squeaked as I went in.

Mr Denny came out of the house, took a cigarette from his overalls, lit it, and squinted at me through the smoke.

'What?' he said.

I went over to him, watching him nervously for signs of anger.

'Jeez,' he said. 'That's crook.'

For a sec I thought he meant it was crook me coming to him for help after the way I'd treated him. Then I realised he was peering at my very short hair.

But I still needed to apologise.

'I'm sorry about the other day,' I said. 'I was worried that if you rescued me, it would make things worse for my dad. I should have explained. I'm really sorry.'

Mr Denny grunted. I took a deep breath.

'I know it's a lot to ask after what happened,' I said. 'But can you give me some advice, please?'

'Yeah,' said Mr Denny. 'Next time you cut your hair, don't use a hedge-trimmer.'

I explained I needed advice about which tool was good for cutting through the bars of a cage.

'A cage?' said Mr Denny.

I nodded. I could see doubt was upon him. I hoped he wouldn't guess that by cage I really meant lions' den.

Mr Denny looked at my school bag.

'Homework?' he said.

Nervously I gave him the smile.

'At least they're teaching you kids practical stuff,' grunted Mr Denny as he rummaged through a big rusty toolbox. 'Here.'

He held up what looked like a pair of garden clippers, but ten times bigger.

'Bolt cutters,' he said. 'Cut through anything, these will.'

I was about to ask if I could borrow them, when Mr Denny's eyes went narrow and behold, he was angry after all.

'The only reason I'm talking to you now,' he said, 'is cos of your mum. She rang me yesterday, poor woman. I feel for her, the strife she's in. But I had to tell her I don't get involved in domestics.'

'It's OK,' I said. 'I'm hoping God will help her.'

Mr Denny snorted.

'Yeah, well,' he said, 'if you want to stay in God's good books you should take a look at yourself, girlie. Dragging people halfway across town on a wild-goose chase. Mucking around with a young bloke's feelings. Not very holy behaviour if you ask me.'

Mr Denny tossed the bolt cutters back into the toolbox.

'Now take a hike,' he said, and went into the house, slamming the door so hard a sheet of rusty metal slid off the roof.

I stood there, looking at the toolbox and wondering what to do.

Kyle came out of the house holding a breakfast bowl. He stayed on the verandah, looking at me.

I went over to him.

'Thanks for the other day,' I said. 'I'm sorry I wasn't very grateful.'

Kyle thought about this.

'No sweat,' he said. 'I got to go up the big ladder. Never done that before. Dad reckons I'm ready to learn cable-greasing now.'

I wasn't sure exactly what that was, but I could tell it must be exciting from the look on Kyle's face.

Mr Denny's voice boomed out from inside the house.

'Kyle.'

'Better go,' said Kyle. 'Um, he's changed his mind about looking for your dad. Sorry.'

I'd guessed that already.

'That's OK,' I said. 'And thanks again for coming to rescue me.'

As Kyle went into the house I was tempted to call him back and ask if I could borrow the bolt cutters.

I decided not to.

What I was planning to do was probably against the law, so best not to get him involved. Instead, on my way out, I just put the bolt cutters into my school bag.

Technically it was stealing, but I was pretty sure God understood.

Chapter 20

On my way to the zoo I learned two useful things.

(1) Outsiders are very kind with directions.

(2) Bolt cutters are even heavier than they look, but it's not so bad if you put your school bag down every five minutes.

Luckily the woman selling the tickets at the zoo wasn't worried about looking in my bag. She was only worried about the time.

'It's four o'clock,' she said. 'We close at five. You won't have time to see much.'

'That's OK,' I said. 'I'm just here for the lions.'

The woman gave me a map and drew an X on it to show where the lions were.

'Thank you,' I said.

'If you need more information,' she said, 'ring our education office any morning after nine.'

I told her I hoped I'd get everything I needed this visit.

'Good luck,' she said.

I went straight to the lions to check how thick the bars of their cage were.

Talk about my lucky day, there weren't any bars, or even a cage.

The lions were in a kind of paddock with trees and bushes. The fence was high, but it wasn't very thick. It was only about three times as thick as a chook fence. I could see it was strong because the lions hadn't bitten through it, but I was pretty sure it wouldn't be able to withstand the ways of bolt cutters.

There was one problem.

The lions didn't look right.

They didn't have enough hair. I know I wasn't one to criticise because I hardly had any myself, but these lions just looked wrong. There were four of them, and not one of them had a thick mane of hair. In every picture I'd seen of Daniel having his faith tested in the lions' den, the lions all had hairy necks.

'Excuse me,' I said to a keeper. 'Are these proper lions?'

The keeper grinned.

I was very tempted to tell him that it wasn't a joke. That God had revealed to me a name tag. That my ordeal wouldn't count if the den didn't have proper lions in it.

But I kept quiet.

'They're females,' said the keeper.

'Oh,' I said.

I thought about this. Female lions would probably be OK. In our church the elders reckoned females weren't as important as males, but things were probably different here in the outside world.

'We had to move the males out to the open-range zoo for a while,' said the keeper. 'One of the cubs isn't well and males can cause problems when there's a sick cub.'

'Thanks,' I said.

I wondered what sort of problems. When I was sick I loved having Dad around. He was brilliant at making healthy drinks and putting frozen peas into socks to cool your head down.

'Don't worry,' said the keeper. 'You're getting your money's worth. I reckon the female lions are the scariest. They do most of the hunting. They're the real killers.'

I didn't ask any more questions.

Just before five o'clock, announcements started coming over the loudspeakers telling people the zoo was closing.

I waited till the crowds had moved towards the exits, then I ducked into a patch of rainforest which I had beheld earlier.

A sign said rainforest was a habitat whose residents were in danger. I knew how they felt. I huddled behind some bushes trying to stay quieter than the quietest rainforest creature.

It wasn't easy. If I moved even a tiny bit, twigs cracked and leaves rustled. I didn't know how jaguars did it.

Luckily the monkeys in their enclosure next door were very noisy too, chattering and screeching and howling. I wondered what they were arguing about. Who got to sleep where, probably, and who'd grabbed the best food, and who was getting the most attention from their parents. They were a bit like the people in our church, getting stressed about what would happen if everybody was allowed into heaven.

I felt sorry for the monkeys, but I was grateful too. They were making even more noise than me. Which meant that even when I rustled, the zoo keepers in golf buggies driving past the rainforest habitat didn't have a clue I was there.

I waited till it was completely dark and I hadn't seen a golf buggy for ages. Then I had something to eat.

The way I saw it, my ordeal was to go into the lions' den, not starve myself to death.

I ate two bananas and some cold sausages. Normally I'd have brought sandwiches, but when I left home that morning I thought my ordeal was going to be in a carwash, so I chose food that wouldn't go soggy.

While I ate, I thought about Mum and the others at home.

I hoped they weren't worrying too much. I'd left

a note explaining I'd gone to sort things out with God, but without any actual details of course.

It wasn't much to make them feel better.

I hoped they'd have faith, like I did.

The bolt cutters were really hard to use. Not only were they very heavy, they were very stiff.

But finally I got the hang of them and lo, Mr Denny was right. They cut through the fence of the lion enclosure like it really was chook wire.

I did about ten snips, just enough to make a flap I could pull back. A flap big enough for a girl to squeeze in, but not big enough for lions to squeeze out. This was meant to be my ordeal, not the rest of the outside world's.

Before I went in, I had a few words with God. I apologised about hurting His feelings, and told Him I wouldn't ever do it again.

'Sorry about the misunderstanding,' I said. 'I've never lost faith in You. Just in the elders sometimes. But not You. Watch and You'll see.'

I pulled back the flap and squeezed through the fence.

'When this is over,' I said to God, 'me and Dad are going to be so obedient You won't believe it.'

I was amazed how much your hearing improves the second you're in a lions' den. Even as I was pushing the flap back into place, the zoo sounds in the night air seemed twice as loud.

Squawking, grunting, squeaking, hooting.

And rumbling.

The lions were awake. I could hear them thudding around in the darkness. But the moonlight was so faint I couldn't see where they were.

I lay down just inside the fence. There was nothing in the Bible about Daniel going up to the lions and introducing himself, and I was sure God didn't expect me to do that.

I curled up on the ground and hugged my school bag and kept as still as I could, which wasn't very still because I was shivering all over.

The grass was damp, but it wasn't just that.

I was terrified.

Terrified of the lions and terrified God would see my fear and think I didn't have faith in Him.

I wanted to run, but I just lay there. When that much fear is upon you, your brain forgets how to do all the normal things.

Breathe.

Pray.

Save yourself.

Then a lion found me.

I heard her footsteps first, padding towards me through the darkness. As she got closer I heard her breathing softly, like she was roaring but in a whisper.

Suddenly she was above me.

Her head and shoulders were huge. I couldn't see exactly where she ended and the dark sky began, but I knew she was most of it.

I tried to squeeze myself into a ball so tiny I'd disappear. I braced myself for mighty teeth to do their worst.

But behold, there were no teeth. Just her huge eyes, staring down at me.

Her breathing rumbled on and slowly a miracle happened.

I started to relax.

I uncurled a tiny bit and stared up into her eyes and it was the weirdest feeling because something about it was familiar.

I felt like I'd been here before. And I could see in her expression that she was feeling the same thing. Which was why she wasn't killing me. And why she was staring down at me with such sadness in her eyes.

Yes, I thought. I'm safe.

'Thank You,' I said to God.

I didn't mean to say it out loud. The words whispered out of me before I could stop them.

And behold, her eyes gleamed and there was a blur. A huge paw moving so fast I didn't fully see it. Just felt it, tearing my flesh.

There was probably a roar too.

But I didn't hear it.

The last thing, the only thing I heard was my own despairing wail.

Chapter 21

There were lots of pretty lights above me.

I knew it wasn't the home-lighting warehouse because the people peering down at me as I lay on the trolley were all wearing white and the home-lighting warehouse uniform was green.

I wondered if I was in heaven.

Then I remembered what had happened. And I knew I wasn't. Grandpop always said that God only invited saved people into heaven.

My brain wasn't working properly, but one thing I knew for certain.

You weren't saved if God let a lion attack you.

I had tubes in me, and pain, and lo, the people bustling around me were saying something about serious loss of blood.

I started to cry.

My head was fuzzy and my hearing had forsaken me and instead of serious loss of blood, I thought they were saying serious loss of God.

Chapter 22

The next time I opened my eyes I was still in hospital and a kind nurse was looking down at me, but this time I could understand what she was saying.

'Hello, Grace. Do you know what's happened to you?'

'I think so,' I said.

'Tell me,' she said. 'So I can see if the anaesthetic's wearing off.'

'Serious loss of God,' I said quietly.

She smiled, but not in a cruel way. She looked a bit like Miss Parry, but with blonde hair.

'Blood,' she said. 'A serious loss of blood. A lion hurt your arm, remember?'

I nodded, which made my arm hurt a lot more. I looked down to see how bad the damage was, but I couldn't tell because my whole left arm was in a bandage and held up by a kind of pulley attached to the bed.

'You needed a blood transfusion,' said the nurse.

'It was a bit dramatic because you've got a rare type of blood and we were having trouble finding enough for you. But luckily your dad is the same type as you.'

I stared.

Not at the nurse, at the figure I'd just noticed standing at the other side of the room. He was in front of the window, so I couldn't see him in detail, just a dark outline against the bright glare of the outside world.

The nurse's beeper went off.

'See you later, Grace,' she said, and hurried out.

I didn't even reply.

I couldn't take my eyes off the figure in front of the window.

'Dad?' I whispered.

'Thanks be to the Lord you're alright,' he said.

But it wasn't Dad. As he came over to the bed, a long wisp of hair flopped over one ear.

I shut my eyes.

I wanted to run, but you can't when you're attached to a pulley. I had to just lie there, feeling sick with disappointment, while Mr Gosper held my good hand in his clammy ones.

'O Lord,' he said, 'we thank you for delivering this child from evil and returning her to her righteous family.'

I tried not to think of Mr Gosper's blood swilling around in my veins. I heard the door open and more footsteps come in. I hoped it was doctors and nurses with a big knockout needle so I wouldn't have to feel this awful.

But it wasn't.

It was Grandpop.

'Praise be,' he said. 'Look at you, young lady. A picture of health.'

'Considering,' said Mr Gosper.

They both nodded, frowning.

'Never again, Grace,' said Grandpop. 'It's over. We promise you'll never be exposed to that evil man again.'

'As God is my witness,' said Mr Gosper, 'he's gone from your life.'

I realised they were talking about Dad. I had trouble breathing. Talking was beyond me. Pulling my hand away from Mr Gosper's was the most I could manage.

'We'll get you out of this hospital as quickly as possible,' said Grandpop. 'In the meantime, Cain and Turk are going to stay with you and make sure you're not bothered by any unauthorised visitors.'

While he was saying this, Cain and Turk clumped into the room, each carrying a chair.

'Is Mum coming?' I whispered.

Grandpop frowned again.

'As you can imagine,' he said, 'she was very upset when she heard what had happened to you. We had to get a doctor to give her some pills to calm her down. She's sleeping a lot, but when you're better you'll certainly see her.'

Mr Gosper took my hand again and squeezed it quite hard.

'I think you owe her peace of mind, young lady,' he said. 'Don't you?'

I didn't reply.

I couldn't.

So this was what serious loss of God felt like.

Cain and Turk sat on their chairs, one on each side of the doorway like prison guards, reading weight-lifting magazines.

I kept my eyes closed and tried not to feel the despair that was upon me.

The nurse came back and took my temperature. She made a sympathetic sound and dabbed the corners of my eyes with a tissue. I wasn't being very successful at not feeling the despair.

I opened my eyes.

The nurse was looking at me.

Concern was upon her.

'Grace,' she said softly. 'Try not to worry if you're having bad feelings or worrying thoughts. That can happen after a big blood transfusion and lots of anaesthetic. You'll probably feel better in a couple of days.'

I stared at her.

I was tempted to tell her I wouldn't. But I didn't because she wasn't trained to treat what I was suffering from, and that wouldn't have been fair on her.

'Thank you,' I said.

'If you're still feeling sad in a couple of days,' said the nurse, 'there's a very nice lady here in the hospital who'll come and talk to you. She knows a lot about what makes people sad.'

'Is she a church elder?' I asked.

The nurse smiled.

'She's a special doctor who knows everything about what goes on inside minds,' said the nurse. 'And inside zoos.'

The moment the nurse left, I started thinking about what she'd said. I thought about it for a long time.

Then I had a word with God.

I told Him the kind nurse definitely proved that outsiders deserved to go to heaven.

I also told God I believed He was as kind as the nurse, and I believed He knew as much about what went on in minds as the special doctor.

'Because You're God,' I told Him.

I pointed out to Him that if He knew what went on inside my mind and Dad's mind and Mum's mind, He must know our faith in Him had never changed.

So why was He punishing us?

'Unless,' I said to God, 'You're not punishing us, and You let the lion attack me for some other reason I don't understand yet because I haven't had a chance to talk about it with Dad.'

I asked God to please let me know if I was right.

If I still had a chance of keeping my family together.
So I'd keep trying.

Just a clue.

A little message.

'Like the kitten,' I said to God.

Chapter 23

The next afternoon I opened my eyes and, behold, I saw a lion.

A small cuddly stuffed lion with a pink mane and eyes that winked. Then I saw whose knee it was sitting on and lo, delight was upon me.

'Dad,' I yelled.

I tried to get out of bed. Dad put his hand on my good shoulder and gently stopped me.

'Easy, love,' he said.

He kissed me on the head and I sank back into the pillows. There was so much to tell him and ask him, but I was still in a sleepy fog.

'Sorry I wasn't here earlier,' said Dad. 'I went to the zoo to thank them for stopping the bleeding and saving your life. They gave me this for you.'

He handed me the cuddly lion.

'I've christened him Daniel,' said Dad.

I saw from Dad's face I didn't need to tell him why I'd gone to the zoo. He already knew.

Which meant he knew I'd failed.

'I tried,' I said sadly, 'I tried to show God He didn't need to punish our family. But He let the lion attack me.'

Dad took my hand in both of his.

'Or maybe,' he said, 'God loves you so much He let this injury happen for a reason. So you won't do anything this dopey again. No more spending nights with wild animals.'

I thought about this carefully, like I always thought about Dad's ideas.

'You mean a sort of reminder?' I said. 'About how He looks after us in some ways, but we have to look after ourselves as well?'

Dad nodded.

'The zoo keepers reckon you were very lucky,' he said. 'The lioness who attacked you was grieving for her sick cub. They'd given her a sedative so they could take the cub away. She was woozy, and they reckon that's why she didn't kill you.'

I could see how emotional and grateful Dad was feeling about that. I was feeling the same and I squeezed his hand.

Suddenly I remembered Cain and Turk.

I peered anxiously at the doorway.

They weren't there.

'Your guards were called away,' said Dad. 'Reception rang telling them their car's being towed away by a red tow truck.'

I stared at Dad, amazed.

'They found you?' I said. 'Mr Denny and Kyle found you?'

Dad grinned.

'Kind of,' he said. 'The minute I saw you on the TV news yesterday morning, I rushed straight here. There was another bloke and his son at reception wanting to see you as well. Claiming it was all their fault. Something about their bolt cutters.'

Alas, I felt awful when Dad said that. Poor Kyle. I'd brought him nothing but tribulation.

'I told them not to blame themselves,' said Dad. 'I explained how you think for yourself, even when you do nutty things. That seemed to cheer them up a bit. He's a generous bloke is Geoff Denny. So's his boy.'

I was glad Dad had stopped them feeling bad.

Looking at him sitting there next to my bed I felt so much love for him, I couldn't stop myself. I threw caution to the wind and hugged him tight. I didn't care about the pain.

Dad hugged me too, then lowered me back onto the pillows.

'You have to be careful with that arm,' he said. 'Don't want you losing any more of our blood.'

I stared at Dad again. And saw that on one of his arm veins was a small scab and a bruise. Relief flowed through my veins. Relief so bountiful I felt dizzy. For I beheld it was my real dad's blood inside me after all.

I hugged him again.

He let me.

'We were lucky,' he said. 'We got it done before Grandpop and the others found out you were here.'

Suddenly I remembered something else.

'That letter,' I said. 'It wasn't from me. I didn't have any idea that Grandpop . . .'

'I know,' said Dad. 'I never thought you did.'

I beheld he was telling the truth because he always did. To me and to everyone.

I lay back on the pillow. All this relief was making me feel a bit weak. And I still had another big worry afflicting me.

'Dad,' I said quietly. 'Don't divorce Mum. You don't have to. We don't want you to.'

Dad stared at me.

'Divorce?' he said. 'I don't want a divorce.'

'Your lawyer rang Grandpop,' I said. 'He told Grandpop you want a divorce.'

'He couldn't have,' said Dad. 'I never asked him to do anything of the kind. I asked him to write a letter to the elders saying I'm prepared to obey the church laws if they let me back in, but he hasn't sent it yet.'

I could see Dad was trying to make sense of all this.

I was too. My mind was churning harder than the Red Sea.

Grandpop had definitely told Mum that Dad wanted a divorce.

And then I realised what must have happened.

And lo, the knowledge hurt almost as much as being slashed by a lion.

Grandpop must have lied about that too.

And it came to pass, even before the shock had completely worn off, that I knew what I must do.

Get me and Mum and Dad and Mark and Luke out of that church.

Forever.

While Dad sat with his head bowed, staring at the floor, I had a silent word with God.

'I don't want to be involved with a church that tells lies,' I said to God. 'Do You?'

I told Him that unless He let me know He did, I'd assume He didn't.

'So,' I said to God, 'our family is going to need Your advice on where to find another church. A kind and loving one that tells the truth.'

Unfortunately, Dad didn't agree. When I told him we had to leave our church, he shook his head.

'We can't,' he said. 'It's not possible for Mum.'

I knew it wouldn't be easy for her, but I told Dad we had to ask her to try.

Dad shook his head again.

'I can't ask her to leave her parents,' he said. 'I'm the one who has to change. If it's the only way to get Mum and you kids back, I'll do anything the church wants. Beg forgiveness, be meek and obedient for the rest of my life, anything.'

The sadness in Dad's eyes made mine fill with tears. But I couldn't persuade him to change his mind.

Dad left just before Cain and Turk got back.

They slumped muttering into their chairs and snatched up their body-building magazines and didn't even notice I was lying in bed cuddling a fluffy pink cheery-faced messenger from God.

They wouldn't have ignored me if they'd known what I was thinking about.

How to get Mum out of the church.

As her choice.

I thought about this for a long time. Finally, while Cain and Turk whispered to each other about protein supplements, I asked God to help me do it.

Well, I started to ask Him.

Then I stopped.

'Sorry,' I said to God. 'Forgot again.'

My arm was throbbing and I had ninety-four stitches in it and I knew I'd probably have a scar for the rest of my life. Which was good. In future, every time I was tempted to sit back and ask God to solve my problems, I'd be able to roll up my sleeve and be reminded of what I'd learned at the zoo.

That God gave us heaven and earth and loving hearts, and the rest is up to us.

Chapter 24

And lo, before I could work out a way of solving our family's tribulations, things came to pass that made the problem even worse.

It was very early morning and I was asleep. So was most of the outside world. But as Dad always said, in our church the bossy boots never slept.

Suddenly I was being shaken and pulled out of bed, and by the time I was half-awake I was staggering along a hospital corridor with Cain gripping one arm and Turk supporting my armpit so he didn't have to touch my bandage.

Nurses were shouting and Uncle Vern was waving sheets of paper at them and threatening to take the hospital to court.

Then I was outside in the chill dawn air and Mr Gosper was opening the rear door of his station wagon and I was being pushed into the back seat.

Mark and Luke were sitting there sleepily in their pyjamas.

'We're going on an adventure,' said Mark.

'Why are we?' said Luke.

Before I could answer, or even work out what they were talking about, I realised Mum was in the front seat.

It felt so good to see her. Tears were upon me.

'Oh, Mum,' I said.

I leaned forward and put my arm round her.

It must have been terrible for her, not being able to visit me in hospital. I knew she'd have a million questions about how I was. She'd want to have a look under my bandage. She'd want to hear about everything that happened at the zoo.

Except so far she hadn't said a thing.

'Mum?' I said.

I leaned forward a bit more.

Mum was asleep. Her seat was tilted back and she was flopped against the headrest, her seatbelt done up tight.

'Let her rest,' said Mr Gosper, getting into the driver's seat.

For a sec I thought that was reasonable. It was very early. Mum probably hadn't had enough sleep either.

But something was niggling me. Mum had never been able to sleep in the car. Not even the time Dad got us lost coming home from Bible camp and we had to drive all night.

As Mr Gosper revved the engine and we sped out of the hospital carpark, I remembered what

Grandpop had said about them giving Mum pills to make her sleep.

I knew what the pills were now.

Sedatives.

Like you give an angry lioness.

I waited till I was completely awake before I started questioning Mr Gosper.

'Where are we going?' I said.

We were already out of the city, speeding along a freeway.

I reminded myself that Mr Gosper was an elder in our church, so what he told me might not be the truth.

'On an adventure,' said Mark.

'That's right,' said Mr Gosper in a fake cheery voice. 'A family adventure.'

I don't usually get car sick, but hearing Mr Gosper describe him and us as a family made me want to spew. I controlled myself. Mum was still asleep, so I was the senior family member for now.

'Where exactly?' I said.

Mr Gosper was watching me in the rear-view mirror. From his face I could see he was trying to decide how much to tell me.

'We're going to the countryside,' he said.

'Why are we?' said Luke.

Good boy, Luke, I thought. Dad would be proud of you.

'You'll see why when we get there,' said Mr

Gosper. 'Now be quiet and look at the view.'

I was quiet for a while, but I didn't look at the view. I'd just noticed something reflected in the mirror. I turned and saw what was in the luggage area behind me.

Suitcases.

Loads of them, piled up to the roof.

This obviously wasn't a day trip.

And that's when I beheld where we must be going. Dad had told me about it once. A farm some of the church members had started. A very remote farm, hundreds of kilometres away from anywhere.

Only the elders knew where it was. The farm people moved out there because they thought our church was going soft. Instead of one service a day and two on Sundays, they wanted three every day of the week. They didn't want TV or computers or telephones or toys. They believed school children should only study the Bible and nothing else.

I felt woe coming upon me, but I didn't let it.

I might be wrong.

'Mr Gosper,' I said. 'I left my toy lion in the bedside cabinet at the hospital. Can we ask them to send it to me?'

Mr Gosper shook his head.

'Better if they give it to another child at the hospital,' he said. 'You won't be needing it now.'

I was right.

We were going to the farm.

But it got worse.

I looked away from Mr Gosper's reflection in the mirror. And saw something that filled me with horror.

A passport, wedged in the car ashtray.

We didn't have passports in our family, so I knew it must be Mr Gosper's.

Our church had branches in about four other countries. I couldn't remember where, but I knew that some of them were even stricter than the farm.

If Mr Gosper kept us hidden at the farm while he got passports for us, and then took us overseas, Dad would never find us.

Chapter 25

I went to the toilet more times that day than any other day in my life.

As we drove further and further away from the city, my tummy got more and more upset.

Not really, of course. Most of the time I was committing the sin of lying. I didn't like doing it, but I hoped God would understand that you can't always be an angel when you're trying to save a family from destruction.

At least Mum didn't hear me.

She slept the whole day.

What I wanted was for us to pull into a petrol station so I could use the toilet. Which would at least give me a chance of getting to a phone.

I had the number of Dad's new mobile written on my armpit in indelible marker. Hidden and indestructible, that's what Dad had recommended. Like our love for God. Even Turk's big fingers hadn't been able to smudge it.

And even if I couldn't get to a phone, there were other people around in petrol stations. If they were kind people like Kyle and the nurse, they wouldn't ignore a girl yelling 'Help, we're being kidnapped and my mum's being given knock-out pills to make her marry a monster.'

But we didn't go to a petrol station, not once. Mr Gosper's petrol tank must have been as big as his bladder.

Each time I asked to go, Mr Gosper reminded me that we didn't use facilities that outsiders used, and stood guard while I squatted behind a tree or in a ditch and faked it.

It was late in the afternoon when I finally thought of a better plan.

I'd probably have thought of it earlier if I hadn't been weak with hunger. That was my fault. People don't want to give you food when you've been going on for hours about having the trots.

OK, Mr Gosper, I thought. If you want us to be a family, you won't mind playing our favourite family game.

'Come on, boys,' I said to Mark and Luke. 'Let's play twenty questions.'

Their eyes lit up. They'd finished the pile of old Bible comics Mr Gosper had brought along, and I Spy was pretty boring when all you could see out of the car window was wheat fields and sky.

I reminded Mark and Luke about our version

of twenty questions. How everyone playing put their minds together and asked the twenty most interesting questions they could think of.

'Mr Gosper,' I said. 'Why can't animals go to heaven?'

'And insects,' said Mark.

'And plastic army soldiers,' said Luke.

Mr Gosper must have been daydreaming, or planning his wedding speech, because he gave a little jump and the car swerved a bit.

Mum's head flopped onto her other shoulder. She mumbled something. I hoped she was waking up and telling Mr Gosper to answer the question, but she mumbled again and stayed asleep.

'Why can't they?' I said to Mr Gosper.

'You're too young to understand,' he said.

'No we're not,' said Mark and Luke.

But I could see Mr Gosper thought we were. Dad wouldn't have liked that. He used to encourage the twins to ask questions when they were only two.

'Mr Gosper,' I said a couple of minutes later. 'If God only wants eleven thousand four hundred and twenty-two people in heaven, why are there six billion of us?'

In the mirror I could see Mr Gosper frowning. For a little while I wasn't sure if it was wrath or genuine thought.

'If you keep asking stupid questions like that,' he said finally, 'it'll be eleven thousand four hundred and twenty-one.'

He chuckled at his own joke.

But I did keep asking questions like that.

Over the next two hours I asked another thirty-four questions like that. And Mark asked three. And Luke did a really good one about whether he could smite Philistines when he grew up.

Mr Gosper got very stressed. Which was my plan. I was hoping he'd get so stressed he'd crack and give up the idea of marrying Mum and turn the car round and take us home.

Alas, he didn't do that.

But immediately after I'd asked my thirty-fifth question, he did something almost as good.

Chapter 26

I asked my thirty-fifth question while we were driving down the main street of a small country town. It was a question based on something Mr Gosper had once told Dad.

'Mr Gosper,' I said, 'why are speed limits only for sinners?'

The speed signs on this street said 50 and we were doing nearly 70.

Mr Gosper turned round and gave me one of those angry exasperated looks adults give kids when they can't stand it any more.

'Look out,' I yelled.

Up ahead, traffic lights were on red and we hadn't even started to slow down. Mr Gosper saw the traffic lights and his eyes went very big.

He stamped on the brake.

There was a loud screech and the sound of a plastic bumper bar being rent asunder and talk about whiplash, our family was saved.

First I checked that Mark and Luke were OK.

They were.

'We crashed,' said Mark.

'Why did we?' said Luke.

I didn't say anything. I decided that when you've just caused a car accident, it's best not to admit it to a four-year-old.

We'd crashed into the back of a pizza delivery car, and the woman driving it was furious. She jumped out and glared at Mr Gosper.

I left him to deal with that. I was busy checking on Mum.

She was awake.

'Where are we?' she said, squinting as if the daylight was too bright for her.

Poor thing. Her voice was slurred and croaky like she'd been on a 48-hour prayer vigil.

Mr Gosper, who was muttering unbiblical things at the pizza woman through the windscreen, ignored Mum and got out of the car.

'We've been kidnapped,' I said to Mum. 'And Dad doesn't want a divorce.'

As soon as I said that, I remembered that Dad had told me how people can only take in one piece of information at a time. Watching poor Mum frown and look bewildered, I could see it was true, specially if they've been drugged.

Mum looked at the pizza car, and then at me and Mark and Luke.

'Are you all OK?' she said.

165

I told her we were.

Mum stared, horrified, at my bandaged arm.

'You're not OK, Grace,' she said. 'What happened?'

'A lion attacked me,' I said. 'Remember?'

Mum concentrated and slowly she did start to remember.

'We're not OK either,' said Mark bitterly. 'Mr Gosper threw our swords away.'

'He didn't say sorry,' said Luke.

'I'm sure we can get them back,' said Mum. 'How long have I been asleep?'

We told her, which made her look bewildered again. Then we all clambered out and had a look at the damage.

It was worse than our previous crash. The pizza car's back window was broken, and liquid was dripping from the front of Mr Gosper's car.

Which was bountiful.

Mr Gosper's car had too much tribulation upon it to drive all the way to the remote farm without repairs, so we had to stay at a motel.

Chapter 27

Mum didn't fully wake up until our pizza arrived, which took ages because at first the pizza shop didn't want to deliver anything to louts from out of town who'd crashed into one of their cars.

Finally the pizza arrived.

After we'd microwaved it and eaten it, and Mum had settled the boys down, I got into bed with her.

Mr Gosper was in the room next door, and the twins were fast asleep, so it was a chance for a serious talk in private.

I started by telling Mum again that Dad didn't want a divorce. This time she understood what I was saying. Though I wasn't sure from her puzzled frown if she totally believed it.

'What about the phone call from Dad's solicitor?' Mum said.

'Grandpop lied about that,' I said.

Mum went very quiet. And that's when I beheld the problem that was upon us. Grandpop was

Mum's father. Nannie was her mother. If we left the church, she'd never see them again.

Thinking about that, and seeing Mum's pale shocked face, made me wonder for one last moment if we'd be better off trying to fix things up with the church.

But I knew we wouldn't be.

'Mum,' I said softly. 'I think Dad's right. I think we have to leave the church.'

Mum bit her lip and I could see she didn't even want to think about that. Fear and doubt were upon her. Poor Mum. I couldn't imagine what it must be like, growing up with a father who's a church elder. But it must leave you very scared about what God might do to you and the people you love if you're disobedient.

'We won't be leaving God,' I said to Mum. 'Just the church.'

She didn't say anything.

'God will understand,' I said to her.

I believed that with all my heart.

'But the church won't understand,' said Mum. 'They'll do anything to stop us. You heard them threaten to take you and the boys from me. They can afford a lot of lawyers.'

'They can't take us if they can't find us,' I said. 'And anyway, Mum, do you want to be part of a church that breaks up families?'

Mum didn't say anything again, but I could see she didn't.

I showed Mum my armpit. I pointed to the motel room phone.

'Let's call Dad now,' I said.

Mum put her face in her hands.

'I need time to think,' she said. 'I need to try and make sense of all this. To talk to God. To be sure I know in my heart the right thing to do.'

I tried to understand, but impatience and panic were upon me.

'Mum,' I said. 'We don't have very much time. Tomorrow will be too late.'

Mum put her arms round me and I could feel her trembling.

'I need God to help me,' she said. 'You know how that is. Isn't that why you went to the zoo?'

I held Mum tight and tried to explain to her what I learned at the zoo. She listened carefully and asked some really good questions. It was just like it used to be before woe was upon our family.

After we finished talking, Mum fell asleep.

I lay next to her for a long time, thinking.

Mostly I thought about the sad trapped look I'd seen on Mum's face for most of the evening. I knew that look so well. I'd seen it so many times, right through my life, whenever Mum thought nobody was watching.

I'd also seen it somewhere else.

In the eyes of the lioness.

I remembered the other look I'd seen in the

169

lioness's eyes, just before she attacked. The proud fearless determined gleam of a mother who'd take on anyone to protect her family.

A couple of times in the last week I'd seen Mum have a flicker of that look too.

As I lay staring at the ceiling, I asked myself a question I'd never asked before.

Did Mum marry the bravest, naughtiest, liveliest-minded man in the church so me and Mark and Luke wouldn't end up like the other church kids?

Bullied. Squashed. Scared to ask questions.

Yes, I said to myself. I think she did.

I slid my arm out from underneath Mum, carefully got up from the bed, went over to the phone, checked my armpit, and as quietly as I could dialled Dad's number.

I held my breath.

A voice answered.

'Dad?' I whispered.

But it was just his voicemail. And before I could leave a message, the phone cut out.

Only for a moment.

Then another voice came on.

'Grace,' said Mr Gosper. 'I want to see you outside. Now.'

Mr Gosper was waiting for me in the carpark.

Wrath was upon him.

'You are a very stupid girl,' he said. 'You think you're clever but you're not. If you had half a brain, you'd have stopped to think how thin the walls of these motels are. How every conversation can be heard if you listen hard enough. Oh yes, and how in these motel family suites there's only one phone line.'

'Mr Gosper,' I pleaded. 'Please don't break up our family.'

Mr Gosper looked at me. His eyes were hard.

'I'm not breaking up your family,' he said. 'I'm saving it. All I'll be breaking is your stubborn will. And when I've saved you and those brothers of yours, and driven the evil from your hearts, God may see fit to reward me. He may see fit to make your mother realise how much holier this family will be with me as your father.'

Mr Gosper opened the rear door of his station wagon.

'Get in,' he said.

There was no point arguing. I got in. Mr Gosper closed the door, locked the car and went back into his room.

Chapter 28

I thought I was dreaming.

A kid with spiky hair was waving at me through a fog so thick I couldn't hear what he was saying.

Then I beheld it wasn't a fog. It was condensation on the inside of Mr Gosper's car windows. I scrambled onto my knees and wiped a clear patch.

And saw Kyle, waving to me to open the door.

'I can't,' I yelled. 'It's got some kind of security lock. The knobs on the inside don't work.'

Kyle frowned. He turned and said something to somebody else.

Mr Denny appeared next to him, peering in through the window.

'Hello,' I said to Mr Denny, trying not to look as shocked and amazed as I felt.

Mr Denny fumbled in the pocket of his overalls, pulled out a piece of wire, jammed it down between the window and the rubber seal, jiggled it about and, lo, the door stayed locked.

Mr Denny muttered to himself, signalled to me to stay in the back of the car, picked up a rock and smashed a front window.

'Did you sleep in here?' said Mr Denny, picking bits of glass out of the window frame.

I nodded.

'It was a bit cold,' I said. 'Mr Gosper wants to get rid of my stubborn will. I think he's trying to freeze it to death.'

'That's child abuse,' said Mr Denny. 'I'm gunna tell *Today Tonight* about that. We got here just in time.'

He and Kyle helped me clamber out of the car.

'See, Dad,' said Kyle. 'I told you we could do this kind of salvaging.'

I saw something glinting over their shoulder. Behind them in the carpark, gleaming in the early morning sun, was the red tow truck.

I remembered where we were. How far from the city. I stared at Kyle and Mr Denny.

'How did you . . .?' I stammered.

'We had your dad over for tea last night,' said Mr Denny. 'When I'd finished showing him my rock crusher, there was a missed call on his phone. No message, just the number of this motel. We drove all night.'

'All of you?' I said. 'Dad as well?'

'He's in our room,' said Mr Denny.

I went wobbly with excitement.

'I like your dad,' said Kyle. 'He knows top jokes for a religious person.'

'Don't get me wrong,' said Mr Denny. 'He's a good bloke. But has he always been this weird?'

They led me to a room at the other end of the motel. Mr Denny opened the door and we went in.

It wasn't weird, it was sort of familiar. In a sad and depressing kind of way.

The room was divided in two. By a sheet hanging from a rope.

'Gav,' said Mr Denny. 'Visitor.'

Dad's face appeared around the edge of the sheet. Then the rest of him.

'G'day, love,' he said, giving me a big grin that didn't quite cover up how miserable he was feeling.

'Hi, Dad,' I said.

I pointed to the sheet.

'What's this?'

I knew what it was, but I was hoping I was wrong.

'I've rigged this up to show Mum and the elders I know the score,' said Dad. 'That this is how I'll have to live at home for a while. Until the elders are satisfied I'm meek and obedient enough. Shouldn't be more than a month or two.'

I felt awful, seeing him like this.

We put our arms round each other.

'Dad,' I said quietly. 'What are you always going on about?'

He didn't answer.

'Being true to yourself,' I said.

Dad still didn't say anything.

Just hugged me tighter.

I buried my face in his chest so he wouldn't see how sad I was. And he held me close so I wouldn't see how miserable he was.

When we'd finished, I saw Kyle was watching us. He looked pretty upset too.

'OK,' said Mr Denny. 'Gav, back behind the sheet. Grace, get your mum in here. Let's get this show on the road.'

Chapter 29

I rushed over to our motel room to get Mum.

But I didn't make it.

As I reached our door, Mr Gosper stepped out of his room. He grabbed me by the wrist.

'Did I say you could leave the car?' he said.

'Let me go,' I yelled.

Mr Gosper tightened his grip.

'This is exactly the problem I mean,' he said. 'Disobedience. And what lies beneath disobedience? A dark and sinful heart.'

'Disobedience is better than lying,' I shouted at him, which I probably shouldn't have done.

Mr Gosper looked at me for a moment, then slapped me across the face.

For a few secs I couldn't see much through my dizziness and tears. Everything was in bright fragments like broken stained glass. When the pain died down and I saw straight again, I beheld that Mr Gosper had raised his hand to hit me again.

But he didn't.

Because somebody grabbed his wrist.

Mum.

She locked eyes with him and for a moment I was back in the zoo.

'Don't ever do that again,' she said to him in a voice that I for one will never forget.

Mr Gosper lowered his hand. But he didn't lower his eyes.

'Only prayer can save this family,' he said to Mum. 'Humble repentant prayer, kneeling before your church, begging forgiveness. Starting with you.'

He grabbed Mum by the back of the neck and dragged her into his room and slammed the door.

I flung myself at the door, but it was locked and I couldn't open it.

'Dad,' I screamed.

Dad and Mr Denny and Kyle came running.

'He's got Mum,' I yelled. 'In there.'

Mr Denny pounded on the door.

'Open up,' he said. 'State emergency service.'

I thought he was just saying that, but he had the plastic ID card and everything. When Mr Gosper didn't open up, Mr Denny dropped to his knees and got to work on the door lock with his piece of wire.

The motel lock must have been a security model like on Mr Gosper's car, because Mr Denny couldn't open it either.

Suddenly there was the roar of a big engine, and

Kyle yelled for us to get out of the way.

I turned and saw Dad driving the tow truck. He was backing it towards the motel door.

'Hook me up to the door handle,' Dad yelled at Mr Denny. 'I'll rip the door off.'

Even Mr Denny looked a bit surprised by that. But only for a moment. Then he attached a loop of cable to the towing hook. He was about to twist it round the door handle when the door gave a click and swung open.

Mum stepped out.

She looked fairly calm, though when I got closer I could see she was breathing heavily.

'It's OK, love,' she said. 'I'm fine.'

She touched my cheek where Mr Gosper had hit me. Then she went over to the tow truck.

Dad got out. They hugged.

'Are you OK?' said Dad.

Mum nodded.

'I'm ready to do that talking now,' she said.

I felt something tugging at my sleeve. It was Mark and Luke. Kyle had them both by the hand.

'Mr Gosper's face is bleeding,' said Mark.

'It's got a big scratch,' said Luke. 'Why has it?'

I turned to where they were pointing. Mr Gosper was in the doorway of his room, holding his cheek, his wisps of hair hanging down.

'It's because he took our swords,' said Mark.

'And because he's a big bully,' said Kyle.

I was about to agree with Kyle, but something

stopped me. It was the expression on Mr Gosper's face. He was trying to scowl at us, but I could see how sad and lonely he was feeling.

Suddenly a thought was upon me. If a church bullies you too much when you're young, perhaps you turn into a bully.

Poor Mr Gosper.

I wished I could have a chat with him. Tell him about some of the experiences I'd had lately. Share some of the things I'd learned.

But before I could take a step towards him, he shut his door.

Mum and Dad went for a long walk, and Mr Denny took me and Kyle and the twins into town for ice cream.

It was only when we were at the cafe table and tucking in that I realised what we were doing.

Outsiders had made the ice cream.

And we hadn't microwaved it.

I didn't care.

While I licked my strawberry ripple, I had a silent word with God. I told Him how well everything had worked out, and how we couldn't have done it without His advice and encouragement.

And His love.

'Thanks,' I said to God.

'You boys are lucky,' said Mr Denny to the twins.

'I know,' said Mark, licking toffee crunch off his chin.

'Why are we?' said Luke, his mouth full of choc-mint swirl.

'Look at you,' said Mr Denny. 'Only four years old and all the adventures you're having. All the new things you're learning. You carry on like this and your folks'll be as proud of you as I am of Kyle.'

Mr Denny ruffled Kyle's hair.

Kyle glanced at me, embarrassed, but underneath I could see he was glowing.

'We are already,' said a voice.

I turned and saw that Mum and Dad had come into the cafe. They were holding hands.

'We're proud of all our family,' said Dad. 'Prouder than we can say.'

'And,' said Mum, 'more grateful than we can say.'

Mum and Dad put their arms round me, their faces shining, and lo, talk about happy tearful hugs, it was the happiest one of my life so far.

'You've got an A-grade specimen there, alright,' said Mr Denny to Mum and Dad. 'Things she's been up to, you wouldn't read about in a book.'

'Actually,' said Mum, 'we're hoping that next time she does a school project we'll be able to.'

Dad gave me a wink.

'That's right,' he said. 'The Book Of Grace.'

Chapter 30

So we left our church, me and Mum and Dad and the twins.

And it came to pass we found somewhere really nice to live, and Kyle and his dad visit us sometimes, and we give them letters for Nannie.

I can't tell you where we are, in case Grandpop and Uncle Vern find out.

But good luck is upon us and things are great and talk about happy families, we're bountiful.

And for that we give thanks every day.

My warm thanks to Tegan Morrison, Dmetri Kakmi, Laura Harris, Sarah Hughes and Tony Palmer.

And to the State Library of Victoria for making their wonderful resources available to me via an Honorary Creative Fellowship.

My gratitude also to the people who enriched my childhood with their loving and compassionate Christianity. Although I don't share their religious beliefs these days, I will always cherish their values.

Morris Gleitzman